The Hennessy Book of Irish Fiction
2005–2015

The Hennessy Book of Irish Fiction 2005–2015

Edited by
Dermot Bolger &
Ciaran Carty

THE HENNESSY BOOK OF IRISH FICTION
First published in 2015
by New Island Books,
16 Priory Hall Office Park,
Stillorgan,
County Dublin,
Republic of Ireland

www.newisland.ie

The story, 'A Vigil', is taken from Andrew Fox's debut collection, *Over Our Heads*, published by Penguin Books and is reprinted here by permission of the author and of Penguin Books.

PRINT ISBN: 978-1-84840-423-6
EPUB ISBN: 978-1-84840-424-3
MOBI ISBN: 978-1-84840-425-0

British Library Cataloguing Data.
A CIP catalogue record for this book is available from the British Library.

Typeset by JVR Creative India
Cover design by Mariel Deegan
Printed by ScandBook AB, Sweden 2015

New Island received financial assistance from The Arts Council (*An Chomhairle Ealaíon*), 70 Merrion Square, Dublin 2, Ireland.

10 9 8 7 6 5 4 3 2 1

New Island would like to gratefully acknowledge the financial support of Hennessy Cognac in the publication of this anthology.

THE EDITORS

Since incurring the wrath of his first editor in 1960 by making Hitchcock's *Psycho* his Film of the Year, veteran cineaste **Ciaran Carty** has been a consistently independent and passionate commentator on film and literature, both as a reviewer and through his internationally renowned interviews in *The Sunday Independent*. A former arts editor in *The Sunday Tribune*, his book, *Robert Ballagh: A Study of the Artist*, appeared in 1986, and *Confessions of a Sewer Rat* – a personal account of his fight against censorship – was published in 1995. Since 1988, he has edited New Irish Writing and chaired the annual Hennessy Literary Awards. *Citizen Artist*, the second part of his Robert Ballagh biography, was published in 2011. In 2013, Lilliput Press published *Intimacy with Strangers: A Life of Brief Encounters*, in which he converses with leading writers, artists, actors and directors on the human condition. Its sequel, *The Republic of Elsewhere: A Cultural Geography*, will appear shortly, to be followed by *The First Time We Met: An A-Z of Cultural Icons*.

Dermot Bolger is one of Ireland's best-known poets and playwrights and the author of eleven critically acclaimed novels, including *The Journey Home* (1990), *The Family on Paradise Pier* (2005) and *New Town Soul* (2010). His twelfth novel, *Tanglewood*, will be published in April 2015. His awards as a playwright include The Samuel Beckett Prize, among many others. His *Ballymun Trilogy* of plays was published in 2010 and his acclaimed stage adaptation of *Ulysses* tours China in 2015, in a production by Glasgow's Tron Theatre. His poem sequence, *The Venice Suite: A Voyage Through Loss,* was released in 2012 and his *Selected Poems* are being published in autumn 2015. The inaugural recipient of the Hennessy Hall of Fame Award, he was named Commentator of the Year at the 2013 Irish Newspaper Awards.

CONTENTS

INTRODUCTION

When I was sixteen, *The Evening Herald* published 'The Devil's Advocate', my first short story. Although I received a cheque for three guineas – a fortune to a schoolboy on six-pence a week pocket money – it was also my last short story. A degree in economics at UCD led to a job on an evening paper in Darlington and later, back to Ireland – by then married with two children – as features editor and film critic on *The Sunday Independent.* By the time David Marcus launched the New Irish Writing Page in *The Irish Press* in 1968 to provide an outlet for emerging fiction, it was too late for the writer I might have been.

Hundreds of writers over the decades have since made their breakthrough in New Irish Writing. The chance to become part of that, albeit not as a writer, came when *The Irish Press,* in difficulties and struggling to survive, went tabloid in 1988 and dropped the page. Vincent Browne (who had lured me to *The Sunday Tribune* to start something similar to a monthly slot I'd initiated in *The Sunday Independent* for new writers, among them Dermot Bolger, Philip Casey and a young barrister called Mary McAleese) approached David Marcus and New Irish Writing found a new home, under my editorship, with David initially involved as a consultant.

The Hennessy Literary Awards, launched in 1971 to heighten critical and popular awareness of the writers discovered each year by New Irish Writing, opened out to include a special prize, focusing renewed attention on poetry in Ireland. Prize money was substantially increased and an overall New Irish Writer of the Year was introduced, the first winner of which was Joseph O'Connor with his short story 'The Last of the Mohicans'. The judges, Piers Paul Reed and Brendan Kennelly, predicted that 'any publisher would put money on him as someone with the potential to become an important writer'. Joe promptly proved them right with his debut novel, *Cowboys and Indians* (1991), based on 'The Last of the Mohicans'.

Hugo Hamilton, Mary O'Donnell, Colum McCann, Colm O'Gaora, Eoin McNamee, Marina Carr, Mary Costello, Mike McCormack and others soon followed him. To mark twenty-five years of the Hennessy Awards, they were brought together in 1995 in the first *Hennessy Book of Irish Fiction,* edited by Dermot Bolger and myself, and published by New Island Books. The book charted the emergence of another generation of young Irish writers, writers we predicted would continue to develop and enrich Irish literature into the next century.

By then, O'Connor had already published a second novel, *Desperadoes* (1994), his short stories, *True Believers* (1991), and a collection of his comic writing, *The Secret World of the Irish Male* (1994), as well as a debut play, *Red Roses and Petrol* (2003). Colum McCann was also quick to follow up on his breakthrough in New Irish Writing with his acclaimed first collection, *Fishing the Sloe-Black River,* in 1994 and a debut novel, *Songdogs,* in 1995. Others took longer to get their chance, but true talent invariably prevails. Mary Costello, whose first story was published in New Irish Writing in 1989, and whose story, 'The Patio Man', featured in the 1995 anthology, only recently got the critical recognition she deserved when *The Stinging Fly* published her first collection, *The China Factory*, in 2012. It was nominated for *The*

Guardian First Book Award, followed last year by her dazzling debut novel, *Academy Street.*

In 2005, ten years after the *Hennessy Book of Irish Fiction,* Dermot Bolger and I edited a second anthology, *The New Hennessy Book of Irish Fiction* – again published by New Island Books – to introduce a fresh crop of emerging writers, not necessarily all award-winners, but all with the potential to build on the promise of their first stories. Many have since become established in various forms of fiction, poetry or criticism, among them Angela Bourke, Claire Keegan, Micheál Ó Conghaile, Phillip Ó Ceallaigh, Paul Perry, Geraldine Mills, Alan Monaghan, Noelle Harrison, June Considine, Karen Gillece, Blánaid McKinney, Kieran Byrne, Moyra Donaldson, Trudy Hayes and Richie Beirne.

It now seems appropriate to publish a third *Hennessy Book of Fiction,* selected from another decade of New Irish Writing, during which we moved to *The Irish Independent,* following the closure of *The Sunday Tribune,* and this year to *The Irish Times.* It is particularly timely, since it also marks the anniversary of a day, two hundred and fifty years ago, in April 1765, when Richard Hennessy – one of the Wild Geese who left Cork to join with the army of King Louis XV of France, before eventually settling in the small town of Cognac on the river Charente – started producing a beautiful, aromatic, amber-orange drink that would become synonymous throughout the world with brandy.

Over the centuries, his family never lost touch with the country he left behind. They cultivated a belief in Irish literature and the unique way Irish writers have with words that, in 1971, inspired their support of New Irish Writing. Their iconic Hennessy Literary Awards are now the longest-running literary sponsorship of their kind in Ireland or the UK.

'The nature of the Irish when they go away is to adapt,' says Maurice Hennessy, a direct descendant, who travels nearly every year from Cognac for the awards, making a point of reading books by the judges and also many of the shortlisted stories, hoping to spot a winner. 'People ask me, why did you not make whiskey? Well, because we were not in Ireland.'

This ability to adapt and to embrace otherness is a characteristic of writers, too. By not quite belonging anywhere, they open eyes to everywhere. Through their creative vision, they confront us with other worlds in a way that seems more real than if we had been there. Their fictions are another dimension of reality, a territory of the mind that overlaps and reaches beyond the actual places we think we know or may take for granted, so that we see everything afresh.

The Hennessy Book of Irish Fiction 2005–2015, which is once again co-edited with Dermot Bolger, owes much to the unwavering support of Anthony Glavin, who edited New Irish Writing during its last two years at *The Irish Press*. It is a personal selection of twenty-five stories from 120 published in the past decade, that in turn were chosen for publication from several thousand stories submitted. Some were winners of Hennessy Awards, others just seemed to fit. Together they reflect a spirit of openness and the power of literature to speak to a culture without borders, a society without divisions.

Ciaran Carty
February 2015

2005

PASSENGER

Alan Jude Moore

Since the publication of 'Passenger' in New Irish Writing in The Sunday Tribune, *Alan Jude Moore has published three collections of poetry, the most recent being* Zinger *(2013). He has also published poetry, fiction and reviews in journals and anthologies in Ireland, the USA and the UK. Translations of his work have been published in Italian, French, Spanish, Russian and Turkish. In 2012 he launched the online literary magazine* Burning Bush 2, *which he continues to edit. His website is* www.alanjudemoore.com.

In his sleep he heard it. Sounded like something had died. Dragged along the tracks, pulling up sharp, wailing first then a sigh drawn back to a stop. Dark outside; rain draped across a body laid down to rest. The line of carriages settled like a necklace into the landscape. It sounded like an animal, the stuttered breath of the engine and the occasional release of fumes from the underside. Out of motion. Newspapers were reopened; or they rested their eyes, stared at the damp black ground that crept up around them. Some rearranged items of clothing, gathered themselves up, like parcels waiting to be sent somewhere they were already supposed to be.

He had been asleep. Dreamt of sitting behind the wheel of his car, of overtaking a slower one, edging into the wrong lane and with a shift of the stick back into the right one. Clear ahead. Dreaming of another man's wife sitting beside him, his hand brushing against her leg when he glided through the gears. Sleeping. Waiting for his destination. He awoke and wiped a patch of condensation from the window with the tips of his fingers. Sitting up, he rubbed his eyes and looked at the woman opposite him. A passenger.

Younger than him, though her lips were giving way to tiny creases that darted into her face. He looked out the window and back at her. Her eyes had traces of mascara and her nail polish was cracked. Blonde hair tight in a ponytail, like his daughter's, like in magazines he found lying around at home. She wore a tight top and, though distracted by the shape of her chest, he kept his gaze above her neck. She lifted herself from a magazine and smiled. He looked at the branches outside, broken and stunted, bobbing up and down in the ditch. He wished she could see him in his car, one hand on the wheel, lights dimmed, heading out clear ahead. Animated.

'We've had to stop,' she said. 'Some trees have come down.'

'Right.'

'They said we shouldn't be long.'

When she spoke he swept his hair back from his forehead and patted down the front of his shirt. He knew several blonde women, some who were even attractive. His wife had gone blonde before their daughter was born but he could not remember what colour her hair really was. His daughter and her friends were also usually blonde. He waited for something to say. At home with his daughter he talked about money. He flattened down the lapels of his jacket.

'I must have dropped off.'

Looking past her he saw children dotted around the carriage, nestled in against the shape of their mothers, eating chocolate and drinking bottles of Coca-Cola. He looked out the window for something in motion, the lights from a plane or a rodent shooting up the bank.

'I suppose we've had some weather,' he said. 'You get that out west though, don't you?'

She put her magazine down on the seat beside her.

'I don't know. I'm from Southampton.'

'Are you on holiday?' he asked.

'I work over here. In Dublin.'

As he listened to her he noticed she had the neutral accent he was used to hearing from receptionists in Dublin and London or anyplace where business was done and people made attempts to imitate elements of the other. She sounded like television.

'Very good,' he said, 'how do you like Dublin?'

An elderly inspector bent over the table. He told them they should be moving to the next station within an hour or two.

'Can't we go back?' she asked.

'Nah, there's a freighter right up behind us. We can't go back. Anyway,' said the inspector, 'the track's damaged. We couldn't go back.' He told them if they wanted tea or coffee, the cart would be around soon and walked through the carriage doors.

'We're stuck here,' he said.

She nodded and tapped her fingers on the table, the tips of her nails making a steady clicking sound. He watched, his eyes moving up and down, from her face to the table, as specks of polish bounced across the laminate, like tiny insects. He noticed her nail varnish was a different shade to her lipstick.

'So, what do you do in Dublin?'

'I'm a dancer,' she said.

'A dancer?'

'Exotic.'

'I imagine it can be.'

She laughed.

'I mean that's what I am, an exotic dancer.'

'Well,' he said, 'you have the figure for it.'

'Depends on my mood.'

He remembered they were stuck in the middle of the country and coughed.

'I suppose it would, whatever you're in the mood for.'

She continued to talk, about the club where she worked, about having to keep in shape, the perfume she wore when dancing and the one she wore outside; how each scent seemed to attract different sorts of men. He kept silent, wondering what perfume she was wearing and what sort of man it meant he was. He compared her scent to that of his wife.

His wife had written a letter to *The Sunday Independent*, a complaint about these clubs. It was one of the things that annoyed his wife and daughter, or seemed to from what he heard when they picked at magazines, reading aloud the quotes highlighted in bold across the pages: Barbie dolls and plastic surgery disaster tits, untouchable virgin whores and sex for sale. He wanted to ask what she would do for money or, at the very least, if her breasts were real.

Refocused above her chest, he looked for signs of ageing. She had a crease at the nape of her neck that he found attractive. He took his mobile from his briefcase. She smiled across the table.

'I should call my wife, let her know what's happened.'

'I suppose she's worried about you?'

'I suppose.'

'Do you travel much?'

'By car usually, it's in the garage and my wife needed hers, so . . .'

He dialled but there was no signal. He slipped the phone into his jacket and said he'd try later. She picked up her magazine, then put it back on the seat when she found nothing worth reading for a second time. Resting her head on the window she let her eyelids fall shut then rebound open again. Eyelashes falling up and down, down and up, her mouth a little open. He stared out the window, watching her movements from the corner of his eye. As she drifted in and out, she looked as young as his daughter. As the lights in the carriage dimmed, he could hardly see the tiny creases and lines around her lips.

Sometimes he overheard his daughter and her friends talking in the kitchen. They compared waistlines and bra sizes, make-up and boys while they thumbed through pages filled with beauty-product advertisements and diets. They were not exotic. Even if they danced, he thought, even if they slipped up and down against a greasy pole in a basement full of smoke and sweat they were not exotic. He thought he should be glad but instead was disappointed with himself, almost angry that his only child was not more interesting. She and her friends were, with a diligence and concentration beyond their years, serving an apprenticeship handed down like family silver by the social standing of those who had brought them into the world. Planned or unplanned. He could not remember. They might all be pretty accidents.

Nine-foot-high posters sold them on everything, from fashion and entertainment to the business degrees they would take in preparation for jobs someone would find for them. His wife made it known that she was incredibly proud of their daughter. He could not tell for what. Their daughter was pretty but for that he thought they should congratulate themselves, not her. He left matters of pride to his wife. She wanted to let their daughter have the collagen job on her lips. It wasn't plastic surgery, she said, it was a minor procedure. Whether he said yes or no would not matter. He could not change the fact that full lips were what she wanted, nor could he change the fact that she would get what she wanted, although perfectly elevated breasts would have to wait until she turned eighteen. The clinic had said so. Until his wife showed him the brochure from the clinic he had not noticed how thin his daughter's lips, like his, really were. Even with his lips he thought she was pretty. It would be a shame then, his wife said, not to make her prettier.

Some teenagers a few seats down turned up the volume on their stereo.

'The Beatles. They were old when I was a kid,' she said.

Swayed by the opening bars of 'Sexy Sadie', he answered yes, they were old. She tapped her fingers on the table. He sat back and listened to The Beatles and the rattle of her rings against the laminate. He thought of the cold air outside, expanding, darker and more frigid, all the way to Heuston Station where his wife would be waiting. He felt the hum of the radiator below him, like the drone from a tuning fork on a wooden counter.

She yawned, stretching her arms over her head, and checked the tiny black stubble on her armpits. She saw him looking at the same place.

'I'm sorry, it's a habit. I have to keep them smooth. For work.'

'No, I'm sorry. I drifted. I mean, I didn't mean to …'

She let her arms slide down to her side and pushed her shoulders back hard against the seat. The Beatles were replaced with a band he didn't recognise.

'I love this song,' she said.

'It's good.'

'They should turn it up, drown out the noise.'

The radiator droned as her rings rattled against the table. The drums seemed unnatural to him, and the rhythm broken. The train jolted forward and he heard the intercom buzz. The train slipped backwards. She lifted her fingers from the table.

'We must be moving,' she said.

'Must be.'

'Is your phone working?'

He reached to check but was interrupted by the inspector moving down, by each set of seats, waking sleeping passengers, telling them they would get to a station soon but the track past it was damaged; a coach would bring them the rest of the way to Dublin. Passengers at the rear were asked to move towards the front, they would be at Clara in five minutes.

'Are you going all the way to Dublin?' she asked.

'My wife was supposed to meet me at the station but she's probably given up and gone home.'

'Do have you kids?'

'A daughter.'

'House in the suburbs, two cars and a dog I suppose.'

'No dog,' he said, 'they don't like dogs.'

He slid his hand into his pocket, reaching again for the phone but took his ticket out instead and waited for the announcement that they had arrived at the station.

The train unloaded at Clara. Like conscripts or convicts, he could not decide, the passengers stepped down. A pair of dogs yelped at the feet of the stationmaster, summoned from the pub to open the car-park gates. The dogs began to bark at the passengers. The stationmaster produced a stick from under his overcoat and lunged at the animal closest to him, the other dashed behind him, sending him reeling in a circle. He raised his stick in the air like a sword. As he prepared to bring the piece of wood crashing down the train jarred and he turned. The dogs broke away from the light of the station back towards the street. People hurried out through the gate. Conscripts, he decided.

Two coaches sat in the car park with the local country and western station blaring from the radio. A magnetic Virgin Mary statuette leaned forward on the dash, loosened with all the going one way and then the other.

She dropped her bag on a seat near the front. As she took off her coat he turned away and excused himself.

'I'm going to sit down the back, try to sleep on the way. The radio keeps me awake.'

'I'll go with you,' she said, gathering up her coat and bag.

As he moved down the rows of seats he saw the sleeping kids from the carriage, or ones who looked just like them. She dropped behind in the aisle, caught between a couple packing their luggage into the racks over their seats. He noticed the absence of her scent as he moved into the back rows. He took a seat by the window, putting his briefcase on the one beside. She was still standing a few rows ahead, shrugging her shoulders, waiting for a gap to emerge. The ticket inspector moved behind her and the aisle cleared for him to make his way towards the back. He lifted the briefcase and sat down.

'I'm sorry, that's kept.'

'First come first served,' said the inspector.

He saw her sitting a few rows ahead, reading her magazine and smiling at a group of children in the seats opposite hers.

'Bastard of a journey this is,' the inspector said, shuffling in his seat.

'I suppose it is, a bit of a bastard.'

'Take the Yanks,' the inspector raised his voice, 'they can shoot a missile from out in the middle of the ocean right in some fucker's letterbox in Iran or wherever …'

'Iraq,' he said, 'it's Iraq this time.'

'… Iraq then, right in some fucker's door and we can't even get a train to make it from one side of the poxy country to the other.'

The inspector turned and stared him in the eye, breathing heavily, ready for a reply.

'Well, they're at war, aren't they?'

The inspector shrugged and rubbed his chin.

'Where are you from,' the inspector asked him, 'England?'

'No. Dublin.'

The inspector said it was the same thing, slid back into his seat and closed his eyes, by the time the coach pulled away from the station he was snoring. There was a change in the air. He had lost the smell of her perfume, her make-up and hand cream. He looked out the window, cupping his hand to his face and breathing in.

His phone picked up a signal again when they were crossing out of Offaly. He shoved it back in his pocket. The Beatles came on, a few rows in front, loud, competing with Big Tom and The Mainliners on the radio. He slipped in and out of sleep through *The White Album.*

He called his wife when they passed through Enfield. She was driving to pick up their daughter from a friend's house. He explained what happened and she agreed to head back into the city and collect him, as long as he wasn't going to be all night getting there. He said he'd try.

The car park in Heuston Station was dotted with family saloons and mini-vans. The passengers disembarked as if they had survived some great disaster, as if they were lucky to be alive. How, he thought, in a country so small could people miss each other so much? He waited until everyone was off the coach. Through the rain and headlights he saw his wife across the road checking her watch. The blonde from the train tapped him on the shoulder.

'Hi. Did you have a good sleep?'

He slipped a little on the edge of the wet pavement.

'Not bad. Travelling makes me tired.'

'It's funny,' she said, 'people seem more tired when they're going home, not so much the other way round.'

'I suppose,' he looked across the road. 'It was nice to meet you.'

'You too.'

'Take care of yourself.'

'Don't worry, I usually do,' she said.

'At work I mean.'

'I know but it's not like that, just . . .' She paused and dragged her bag higher on her shoulder.

'Just what?' he asked.

'Come down and see sometime.'

'Maybe.'

'Come for the music.'

'Why, is the music good?' he asked.

She smiled and said he'd like it.

A taxi pulled up quickly when she raised her arm in the air. As she moved off towards the car he asked her name but was drowned out by the noise of engines. He saw her waving to him as she sat in the backseat. He waved back and, through a break in the traffic, crossed the road to his wife.

'Who was that?'

'Someone from the train.'

'Were you giving her directions?'

'No,' he said, 'just talking.'

'About what?'

'Music, we were talking about music.'

He heard the low hum of the engine as he approached the car; his wife was asking more questions about the blonde he'd been talking to, what was her name, where was she from, why were they talking about music. He could have answered some but leaving others unanswered would result in more questions. He walked around the car and saw his daughter sitting in the back, lips swollen, unable to speak. He climbed into the passenger seat and turned up the radio.

'Does that have to be so loud?' his wife said without looking at him.

'It helps.'

Tapping his feet to a song he didn't know, he cupped his hands to his face and took a deep breath. He wiped a small patch of condensation from the window with his fingertips and rested his head back on the seat, the lapels of his jacket up around his chin. The car pulled into the line of headlamps and tail lights beginning to stretch along the road from the station out of the city. The indicator lights ticked; their machines merged into an incandescent streak pushing through the rain.

'It helps,' he said, 'drown out the noise.'

BEACHED

Jennifer Farrell

Jennifer Farrell lives in Chapelizod. She studied at NUI, Maynooth as a mature student, where she received an MA in Modern History. Following her New Irish Writer of the Year Award for her first story, 'Beached', she won the inaugural Memoir Competition at Listowel for her childhood memoir, The Girl in the Wardrobe *(2012). She is currently working on short stories and an idea for a crime novel.*

In a terrible fluster, Alice pulls everything out, roots down to the bottom of her bag, turns it upside down, a jumble of odds and ends tumble out; crumpled tissues, cotton-wool, safety pins, deodorant. It's not there, the blue and white box, no loose tablets either, among the junk. It was always a mad rush on Saturday night, before Eddie arrived on the dot of 8.30. He didn't like to be kept waiting and was liable to moan if she wasn't ready on time.

'Women!' he'd say to no one in particular. 'Bloody women!'

It was stupid, forgetting the painkillers; her head is splitting, a dull throbbing, inside her skull.

The after effects of the vodka and orange, no doubt. The car smells of vinegar and semen and cigarettes. Chip papers are bunched up on the floor, brown and sodden and greasy; crumbs of fish batter and spiceburger litter the car mat. Alice is cold, she pulls the car blanket up to her chest, wraps her scarf twice around her neck and wriggles into her tights. Lighting up a cigarette, she spots something in the distance. Another car further down the beach is pulling off, she watches the tail lights disappear over the wooden bridge. Surely they weren't the last, she hates being the last.

The beach is empty now, the sky pockmarked with clusters of fading stars; out along the coastline the harbour lights of Dublin Bay are starting to wane in the gathering light. The Docklands development is visible, with the new apartments and glass-fronted office blocks that have sprung up and altered the landscape since herself and Eddie started coming here. They stretch outwards towards the Irish Sea, eerily lit with low-voltage light bulbs. Above them, she can make out the faint dark shapes of cranes, with outstretched arms. Horrible. Like Meccano or Lego, Alice thinks. She opens the car door, pushes out the smoke. A fresh, easterly breeze is like a tonic on her face. She looks at her watch.

'Eddie, it's ten past six,' she says shaking Eddie's arm.

'Are ya right, Eddie, the guards might come!' she shouts into his ear. Eddie's head swings sideways like a pendulum; he mumbles something incomprehensible, before dropping his head to his chest again, and presently he starts to snore.

'Jaysus, Eddie, have a heart, I'm frozen, all the other cars are gone; hear me! Hear me! Wake the fuck up.' She elbows him in the arm, slaps him under the chin, about the face. Eddie is slumped in the driver's seat, bits of blue polka-dot boxer shorts showing through his open fly, his shirt bunched and twisted around him. She flings the butt out, watches the red glow as it drops in the sand. In the distance, she sees the lights of the car ferry, going towards Alexandra Basin. The Holyhead ferry, she thinks, the Irish woman's answer.

Almost a quarter of a century ago, '79 it was – the year of the Papal visit – a bitter, cold night, six weeks before Christmas.

An overnight stay in Liverpool, in the B&B they'd said was cheap enough, if you couldn't afford to stay at the private clinic. Five Irish women, there were, that night for the clinic. They all boarded the bus at the quayside, all were travelling alone, two were married women, Alice later found out.

In the aftermath of the Papal visit, an aura of angelic holiness ensued; the churches packed out every Sunday, queues for Holy Communion.

Staff at the Family Planning Clinic were cautious; all hush-hush it was back then, like the Secret Service. From a coinbox around the corner, Alice phoned Liverpool. The female voice at the other end was brisk; she asked how far was she into the pregnancy, quoted a price in sterling and told her to phone back the next day. Panic stricken, and with no savings, her only option was to arrange a high-interest loan from a local loan shark. Two years it took her to pay back that loan, two years of hard slog in Woolworth's café; barely covered her expenses and boat fare when she bought the sterling. She'd told her mother it was a shopping weekend, for the cheap Christmas presents.

Alice adjusts her seat to the recliner position. Christ, the thought of what she went through in that kip in Liverpool; trolleys lined up, head to foot in the corridor, herself with a heavy cold from the crossing, so they couldn't give her a general anaesthetic. The protesters outside the clinic, when the bus arrived, waving placards and chanting abuse.

'Take no notice of the Jesus people,' the bus driver advised, but it was easier said than done.

'Them *nutter's* are here every day,' he went on. 'Act like you don't see them. Upstarts, they are, religious freaks and bible-bashers, nothin' but trouble.'

He gave the protestors the two fingers.

One woman was on her knees, holding up a crucifix, another was shaking huge Rosary beads, like some voodoo witch. Alice looked down as she squeezed through, not wanting to meet their eyes, or see the terrible posters of what they claimed were aborted babies.

From inside, she could hear them praying.

She can never forget the heckling and jeering, afterwards.

'Murderers!'

'Sinners!'

'Baby-killers!' they taunted, as the bus pulled away. There was no mistaking the collective hatred in their eyes as they surrounded the bus.

'Are you absolutely certain about this procedure; would you like to give it more thought?' the nice-looking doctor had asked in the cubicle she was brought into to have her blood pressure checked.

'You could wait till your cold is better, have a general anaesthetic.' He smiled, showing even, bright teeth. His smile was genuine, Alice knew, and if only she hadn't been in this bloody state she'd have fallen head over heels for him.

'I'm sure,' she said.

They didn't bring the consent form till she was waiting outside the theatre, in a line of trolleys.

'You'd be surprised how many change their minds at the last minute,' the nurse said cheerily. She'd scribbled her signature and was pulled in. It was all hustle and bustle in there, a sharp smell of disinfectant, glaring lights, masked and gowned figures moving about. The mild sedative they gave her didn't quell her anxiety. She had the jitters, her knees rattled, as they strapped her feet up in stirrups and injected her vagina with local anaesthetic; Alice closed her eyes, took deep breaths like she was told, prayed for courage and forgiveness to all the angels and saints she could remember. She cried out, it seemed her insides were being pulled out. There was a plopping sound. More poking and prodding and pulling and dragging, with whatever it was they were using on her. She'd tried to raise her head, to look down.

'Try not to move, we're almost there,' she was told.

'You're oozing a lot, how many weeks are you?'

'About nine weeks, maybe ten,' Alice mumbled.

'Have you sanitary towels with you?' the nurse asked, pulling back her mask.

'Yeah. Back in the ward.'

'You need to rest for a bit;' she said, taking everything away in two kidney dishes.

'If all goes well, you can leave in a couple of hours.'

She remembers there was a lot of blood; they took a while cleaning her up. The next trolley was pulled in; Alice couldn't see the girl's face, only the white cap on her head. She was taken into a recovery cubicle where another nurse stuffed wads of cotton wool between her legs and gave her a clean gown.

'All done now, don't be worrying yourself,' she said, in a friendly Liverpool accent.

'You'll bleed for a couple of weeks, be sure to get your check-up back in Ireland.'

Pushed in and pulled out; cleaned out, like a bloody roasting chicken.

The pain after, and an overwhelming feeling of relief, is what she remembers most. And the sobbing of some girl in the next cubicle. Crying was healthy, the friendly nurse said, but Alice couldn't cry.

It was quiet in the bus going back until the driver switched on the radio and that crappy pop song blared out: 'Video Killed The Radio Star'. To this day Alice hates that song. The sickly smell of fried onions in the B&B made her want to throw up. In an up-beat, artificial voice, the landlady announced they could have dinner for a bit extra; liver and onions with mashed potatoes, chicken soup for starters. Her dress was yellow and flowery, she had pink lipstick painted garishly over her top lip to give an impression of a cupid's bow.

Alice picked at her dinner; all she could manage at breakfast was a bowl of cornflakes with a cup of weak tea. The two at her table were only about eighteen or nineteen, country girls who'd travelled miles by train to Dublin.

One of them told her she was studying for her Leaving, her fella gave her the money, she said. He got a tax rebate, as luck would have it, from the Revenue.

If Alice's mother suspected anything, she never said; she never even mentioned the missing Christmas presents. Things went back to normal, the mundane pattern of her life continued. After taking Monday off, Alice was back behind the counter of Woolworth's café, serving up sausages and mash that Tuesday. There were one or two weeping sessions in the ladies, but no one suspected anything at work. She used Paddy Pads nappies to soak up the blood, she took a lot of Phensic.

Christmas came and went. It was 1980; the loan shark called every Friday evening on the dot of 7.

She'd be twenty-five now, Alice thinks, striking a match. It's always a girl, when she thinks of it; a dribbling one-year-old in a pink party dress, a cheeky ten-year-old with pigtails, a pimply, teenage rebel with no cause at fifteen.

Would she be a beauty at twenty-five? A daughter would have been nice, Alice thinks.

Eddie doesn't know, men could be cruel about such things; the less they know the better is her motto. There was no one special before Eddie. Not being the romantic type, Alice's encounters with the opposite sex have been limited to a series of one night stands. She's lost count of the men she's met in the night-clubs in Leeson Street and Baggot Street. Twenty-somethings and thirty-somethings and forty-somethings, all with that same look after a few drinks. That one in '79 was fatal, a medical student celebrating his exam results. Ended up in some hole of a bedsit in Rathmines, woke up with a splitting headache, bottomless, except for an oversized striped pyjama top. She remembers a dark sleeping head next to her on the floor. Nice-looking chap when he turned around, to give him his due. Very classy and mannerly, she'd thought; even made her tea and toast before he left.

'Make yourself at home,' he'd said, 'have a kip if you want, my flatmate won't be back till after six, as long as you're gone by then. Have to meet a few heads,' he'd said, 'in Davy Byrne's. Exam celebrations, you know the score.'

In the doorway, he blew her a kiss.

'*Ciao*,' he'd said in a mock Italian accent and closed the door quietly.

She never saw him again. It was her first and last Trinity student.

Her predicament became clear after a few weeks. Self-denial was her first reaction. Her job at Woolworth's café was all they had, along with her mother's pension to keep the wolf from the door. Lying to yourself wouldn't pay the bills. Could they have managed, she sometimes wonders.

Streaks of pinkish light appear out at the horizon, the hoot of a ship's horn. Alice looks towards the lighthouse. The car ferry has passed into shore. Eddie is still snoring, jerking peevishly like he's having a nightmare. She stuffs the wads of toilet roll into her bag, throws the empty vodka bottle onto the back seat. Oh, what she'd give, to be in her bed, with her hot-water bottle and her flannel pyjamas on. She'd take a couple of Panadol, have a nice lie-in, get the evening Mass.

Alice and Eddie are together almost eight years now, they go out once a week, the beach is their special place. Same every

Saturday; The Horse and Hound for a few drinks, the chipper and the beach. They aren't the only ones, and the guards turn a blind eye, except if there's trouble. Eddie is no skinflint, buys her drinks and chip suppers, they listen to 'Night Train' on the radio, cover themselves with the car rug.

It's the *pits* waiting for Eddie to wake. Watching the dawn break, listening to his snoring, things have a way of coming into sharp focus, like a tell-tale photograph. Her life seems tacky, a holy show to be precise; almost fifty and still living at home, still arsing about in a car on a beach.

Needing to spend a penny, Alice squats down behind the car. A seagull watches with beady eyes from a nearby rock, the white-grey of its feathers vivid in the emerging light. Further out, the sound of waves, lapping quietly over the shingle.

Back in the car Alice throws out the chip papers, the gull squeals as a carcass of ray-bones is lifted into the air, bits of batter and chips fall from the bag.

Stretching her legs, she settles back.

She can't complain; the tiger economy has been good to Eddie, he's still doing well at the building. The car he drives now is a swanky-looking red hatchback, with recliner seats and plenty of leg room. You'd have to be a contortionist for that other yoke he had, with the bucket seats; nearly broke her leg one night. Eddie is well travelled; sowed his wild oats in the farthest regions of the globe. Like something out of a thriller it is the way he tells it. The exotic places he's been to in his youth. The stories of adventure he'd shared with her; the women he'd had in Russia and Thailand and Africa; up-front is Eddie about his sex life. The sixteen-year-old beauties, doing tricks in doorways near the Kremlin, for a few rubbles; black broads, in South Africa, with behind's on them like hippos; and the elfin-faced Thai girls swinging out of brothel windows, some of them no more than twelve or thirteen.

Alice licks a tissue, rubs at the caked-in mascara under her eyes; without make-up her eyes have a bewildered sleepy look. She wonders what she'll wear next Saturday.

Eddie gives a sudden snore, jerks his head up. 'What the fuck!' he grunts, doing up his fly. 'What time is it?' Alice feigns a yawn, fingers up her hair in the vanity mirror.

'Fuck sake, Eddie, just drive us home,' she snaps.

Eddie starts the car.

2006

PAGODA

Thomas Martin

Thomas Martin was a student at Trinity College when 'Pagoda' was published. He has gone on to become a successful screenwriter. He was awarded the Sundance Institute's Alfred P. Sloan grant for promoting science in film, has been Writer in Residence at the Irish College in Paris, and has worked on top television dramas for RTÉ and the BBC.

Simon leaned against the motorcycle and watched from the track as Tilda knelt on the forest floor. She had her back to him and was carefully adjusting the aperture on her camera. They had stopped so that she could take a photograph of a gigantic tree, a monster whose bark fell over the crumbling wall of an ancient Khmer ruin, its wood split like some leviathan hand pulling the building back into the bush, reclaiming it for the jungle. Simon curved the blade of a Swiss army knife around the edge of a thick aloe vera leaf he was holding in his hand, squeezing the sap onto his forearm and rubbing its jelly into his skin. He didn't take his eyes off Tilda.

The rain came suddenly, clapping against the canopy high above them, loud as applause in a packed theatre. It lasted only a few moments but it was startling and made her turn from her photography. She stood up, facing him with a look of wonder, and almost smiled. He was breathless for a second, struck by what a beautiful mess she was, her hair partially stuck to her forehead with sweat, her knees muddy below the hem of her shorts. The jungle affected him, the smell of the trees, the moisture. It stirred him to look at her in it. He picked up the water canister and stepped away from the motorbike, moving from the track onto the thick mulch toward her. Tilda watched carefully as he stopped to shake large drops from a fern and onto his face, wetting his lips.

He handed her the flask, which she took, his fingers lingering over hers. Simon leaned forward as she drank, his head slightly behind hers, his fingers gently touching the inch of exposed skin between her T-shirt and the waistband of her shorts. With a slightly open mouth, he brought his lips down against the nape of her neck. But they burned with the sharp bitter taste of her and he drew back, putting his fingers to his mouth, which tingled all over. Tilda had sprayed fresh DEET onto her neck and arms when they had stopped last. The acrid taste of the mosquito repellent left the skin on his lips stinging. She shoved him out of the way and walked stolidly back to the motorcycle.

'Come on, Simon. That rain could have messed the roads. It might be just dirt tracks to the Pagoda for all we know. And the sun will be setting soon. I can't miss that. Do you even know how far away we are?'

'Out here, it feels like we're the only two people left in the world,' he said.

She laughed derisively.

'What a cheap line. You're such a juvenile sometimes. You think you can *fuck* me here on the forest floor and all is forgotten?'

He looked blankly back at her. She frowned, raised her camera to her face, and shot him standing there in front of the ruin and the tree.

The drive was fast through the jungle; the path was well worn and relatively dry from the cover of the trees. But the jungle gradually fell away and then it was just a track through miles of watery fields that ran north of Preah Vihear and to the horizon, Laos.

The rain had tinged everything brown. His eyes had to seek out the sporadic patches of green reeds in the rice fields that flanked them for miles. They passed a few huge oxen, bags of skin and bone, wading through sludge, chewing and swatting mosquitoes from their hides with the brushes of their tails. He squinted into the distance, the brown and red colour seemed to evaporate into the sky and his focus blurred for a moment. His scarf was pulled tightly over his nose, flecked with mud. The driving was becoming slow, hard work. He struggled with the motorcycle, shifting his weight to keep them balanced as he weaved around the stagnant ponds of rainwater that were becoming larger as they got farther along the dirt road. It was completely washed over in places, steam rippling off it, submerged rocks sending shudders through the handlebars and into his body. The air was heavy and he couldn't maintain a straight line long enough to build pace and create a breeze. There was an agoraphobic sparseness to the surroundings that made him long for the cover of the rain forest. The wheels turned slow revolutions, flicking streaks of red and brown dirt against their legs.

He felt her arms move around him. She had been holding back until then, carefully clasping the back bar, trying not to touch him, holding her legs out from his body like wings. But now she moved onto him, wrapping him in a backwards embrace, her bare legs slicked with mud, straddling him from behind as her hands moved across the front of his chest and clasped each other, locking over his belly. Her body was warm against his. The sensation of her breath on his neck was intoxicating after the days they had spent apart. Maybe she had forgiven him, he thought, or maybe she was just as achingly tired as he was and was giving in, a tight knot uncoiling.

Simon clung to the idea of forgiveness and it urged him on. He managed to build up speed by staying riskily close to the edge of the ditch. Then he caught sight of the hill in the distance.

Everything had become dull, the colours washed out in the rain, and he had to strain his eyes to see it. The plan had been to reach the hill and climb to the top where there was a small Pagoda from which they could watch the sun set over the rice fields of northern Cambodia. He had glimpsed it from the corner of his eye. Hypnotized by the horizon, the Pagoda had emerged from the landscape like a secret from one of those trick paintings you have to stare at to see the second image. For a moment the road became the sky. The front wheel turned suddenly in a jack-knife but the bike kept moving forwards, the wheels turning slower than they were travelling, almost gliding on top of the hot muck. The brakes had lost traction. In a second her arms were gone from him, the motorbike vanished from under them and everything was red and brown mud.

He raised his head from the road. Dirty water streamed from his hair, staining his neck and the collar of his shirt. The bike had slid four or five metres in front, the tyre tracks sweeping a wide-berthed pattern in the mud. It lay half submerged in the ditch, the front wheel up and spinning. Simon pushed himself upright. He looked around but couldn't see her. Turning in a circle, he said her name then shouted it as he ran back along the road, skirting the ditch in a panic. Then he saw an arm and a leg grappling against the edge of the ridge that ran down into the water of a rice field. It was a four-foot drop into the rancid stagnant dyke. Tilda was struggling to haul herself out of it, clutching a root protruding from the side. The water moved with a thick layer of mosquitoes that burst into a cloud as his foot sent a rock in with a splash. His heart skipped when he saw the long sleek body of a snake just under the surface of the liquid. He quickly curled his arm around her waist and rolled her back onto the road. Their bodies lay tangled and panting.

He sat up and held her face. Tilda's eyes opened and she groaned.

'Are you alright?' he asked as he moved his hands carefully over her, checking her bones.

'I'm fine, I think,' she replied, rubbing her head as she pushed herself upright.

'Are you sure?'

'Your eyes are frightened,' she said.

Simon's lip was bleeding. Tilda put her fingers to it and softly smudged the blood around his lips. They both had their hands on each other's faces and she leaned in to kiss him but stopped. Remembering that she was supposed to hate him now, she pulled away and covered her face with her hands and started to cry. Her shoulders heaved under the sobs. Simon reached his hands to hers but she flung them from her face, clenching her own into fists. Her eyes were red, two tears cutting a clean line on her cheek. He fell back deflated and they sat on the muddy road looking at each other.

'I'm sorry,' he said.

'Don't. Just don't. Your apology is hollow.'

'I feel terrible but I can't go back in time. I can't just wash everything away.'

'Your sins you mean? Well maybe you should try bathing in something cleaner, you bastard.' She flung a fistful of dirt at him. It slugged him in the shoulder, his whole body dripped with it anyway.

'So where do we go from here?'

'That's the question isn't it? Do you want to go back, Simon? Do we turn back now?' Her eyes were searching. He knew how loaded her question was, how many directions it moved in. She didn't want to go back. Always move forwards was her philosophy. He looked to the ominous sky. The clouds were so grey and black in places that the sun could have set behind them and night could have arrived without them noticing. If it rained again, the roads would be awash and he wouldn't be able to get them home in the darkness. He wasn't even sure if the bike had survived the crash, or if they had. And there was a storm coming. If the Pagoda wasn't habitable, they were in trouble. But maybe they had gone too far to turn back now. Simon was confused. He closed his eyes and thought of going right back, undoing everything. He imagined the road being sucked back into the wheels, retracting the journey downriver, the smell of the open sewers of Phnom Penh rushing out of their noses, across the border to Vietnam, Saigon again but backwards, conversations of betrayal unspoken, the tides of Munet go in and out in reverse, the phosphorescence dissolves into the water, he pulls himself out of her in the moonlight, the kites in the square at Hué drop from the sky, his beard disappears into a skin that is lightening, an old man takes the Japanese military-issue Honda from him and hands him 1,000 US dollars, then into the air and down, spit coffee out into a cup at Frankfurt airport, into the air again and moonwalk out through the gates at Heathrow, let go of her hand and swallow the words – *let's stay away for ever.*

'It's your choice. Are you turning back?' she said. 'We can drive to Siem Reap. I can sell the bloody bike. You can go. I can give you money for your ticket home, or wherever. If that's what you want Simon. Is it?'

He kept his eyes closed and shook his head.

She stood looking into the ditch as he used all his weight to wrestle the bike upright. He kicked the pedal start a few times and it choked and spluttered on. A five-foot cobra floated on the surface of the still water. It had been dead at least a day. Flies moved back and forth in frenzy over its decaying head.

The sky was getting darker as they pressed on. Simon heard the grumble of thunder in the distance. He flicked the lights, which blinked a few times before staying on.

There was a clutch of houses at the base of the hill. Some were no more than huts covered in straw. All stood on high stilts of wood lifted from the flooded fields. They were huddled under the sparse protection of some palm trees whose thick fans of leaves moved in the wind, high above the dwellings. Groups of half-naked children spilled from the gaps and the cracks in the structures and rushed the light of the motorcycle. They repeated 'Halo, Halo,' over and over, their small hands reaching out and touching Simon's arm. As the children begged for alms, adults watched from a distance. Simon looked at their homes, wondering how the weak-looking buildings didn't get washed away in the monsoon. Tilda made faces and played with the children who ran about her, their bellies bloated with malnutrition. They laughed and pointed at the two strangers who were almost red as the mud dried and turned to clay against their skin.

Concrete steps had been built into the side of the hill because it was so steep at the base. He didn't try to help her up the large steps and went ahead, his eyes searching out the path that twisted around the side of the mound like a smile. The higher they climbed, the rockier and muddier it became. A couple of local men with a goat passed them. One stopped and pointed at the sky before making motions of rainfall with his fingers. Simon looked at the man's badly mangled hand.

By the time they were within eyeshot of the Pagoda large drops of rain were falling periodically. Simon took his rain poncho out of his bag and tossed it to her. She had forgotten hers and offered a half smile in thanks.

The grey had disappeared from the skyline. There were streaks of black cloud laid like smoke now, upon a sky that seemed suddenly to be a brilliant white. The landscape spread before them, an expanse of green and brown. They watched the flooded rice fields, laid flat like shards of glass, stretch into the horizon, all the way to the snake of the Mekong Delta.

Then the thunder clapped its huge booming presence. The dead heat was about to break, the earth was gasping for it. They made it to the gate of the simple Pagoda just in time and rushed under a small wooden shelter, an observation deck that looked out over the land. Tilda was breathing hard with the exultation of racing the storm. The hood of the poncho had blown back from her face.

There was a plant growing against the side of the shelter. Its flowers were in bloom and the petals fell in tassels over the awning in a thick waterfall of red.

'It's like that plant you used to grow back home in the greenhouse,' she said, holding up a portion in her hand. 'What was it called again?' He knew she knew the name but was making him say it.

'It looks like an *amaranthus*.'

'But the garden name?'

'Love-Lies-Bleeding,' he said, 'but it's South American. I don't think it grows here'.

Simon turned away from her and pulled a handful of the plant aside like a curtain so that they could look across the courtyard to the temple. A boy, no more than seventeen, had appeared in the doorway of the wat. He had the bald head, the drooping ears and the serene face of a siddhartha. His skin was a deep golden honey against the bright ochre *lungi* that was wrapped loosely about his body. The thunder came again, loud and near. Then the sky opened. Its white colour was turning orange and was blood red around the edge of the black storm cloud. Simon looked from the boy to the eerie skyline. It was as if the sun were being smothered rather than setting. The rain got harder and harder, huge and unrelenting.

The young monk stepped out into the blur of the courtyard and walked to the centre. The cloth of his robes slapped tightly against his skin as it soaked up the flood, beads of water rolling off his head. They watched him as he stopped by a small stone stool and placed something on top of it. He opened his hands as if in prayer and raised his face to the onslaught of the water. Then he began to turn slowly, unwrapping his cloth. He let it drop to the ground revealing a toned, youthful body and picked up the small object from the stone. It was soap. He moved the bar across his nakedness, building a thick white lather on his skin, letting the rain water wash it off.

Simon was engrossed, and then surprised as Tilda grabbed him to her. She unbuttoned his shirt and pulled it from his back. Holding the garment in her hand, she pushed him from the protective shelter, leaving the stain of a muddy handprint on his shoulder blade. He stood in the open and looked across the courtyard to the monk, then back to Tilda. The rush of water was suddenly all around Simon, drenching him. Tilda watched as it beat hard against him, a white skin emerging as rivers of red dirt ran off.

EARTH

John Murphy

John was shortlisted in the Hennessy First Fiction category for 'Epiphany' (now renamed 'Earth') in 2006. His poetry collection, The Book of Water, *was published by Salmon Poetry in 2012. In 2013 he was a prize-winner in the international Bridport Prize. In 2014 he was a finalist in the RTÉ Guide/Penguin Ireland competition. He is a theoretical computer scientist by profession and lives in Dublin.*

Patrick Timmons had decided to take a sick day from his job at the Dublin Gas Company. He would have breakfast with his wife and two boys and then take a walk in the Phoenix Park. Later, he would spend the day drinking in Stoneybatter with his brother-in-law, Frank.

He and the boys chattered noisily as they ate. In contrast, his wife Margaret ate in silence, anticipating the events of the day. She knew he would not go to work today.

He left the house shortly after ten past nine and walked to the top of Ross Street and passed between the greens that led to O'Devaney Gardens. From O'Devaney Gardens, he turned onto the North Circular Road and continued his walk to the Phoenix Park. He walked as far as the dog pond and sat down on a green bench and lit a cigarette. He inhaled deeply and his reverie was interrupted by a series of sharp coughs. His doctor had told him to quit smoking but Patrick Timmons would never give them up. Getting out of the bed each day at 7.30 a.m., he would light his first cigarette of the day. He smoked all through the day and, in the evening after his dinner, the tiny living room of the house on Ross Street filled with smoke. At bedtime he would always tell the boys a story and this was when he was at his happiest. On the double bed adjacent to the children's bunk beds, he would stretch himself out and light a cigarette. In the darkness he would gesture with it as though it were a wand of light illuminating the story as it unfolded itself from the matrix of his imagination.

The children loved his stories and every evening he tried to tell a different one. Sometimes, he would tell a new story but with characters from an older story. Often the children demanded to hear a story that he told them before. A great favourite was a story concerning a man who fought and beat the biggest bully in his town. The hero had no first name and the children would simply say: 'Tell us about McGuff, Da.'

Each evening he cycled home from the pub with his coat tied by a piece of string and smelling of smoke and drink. In spite of this the boys were always glad to see their father. Once, his eldest son asked him outright, 'Are you drunk, Da?' and he had replied, 'No son, I'm just tired that's all. I just feel a bit sleepy.'

Timmons put out his cigarette butt on the pavement and walked to the Parkgate Street entrance of the park. From the park entrance he walked through Arbour Hill, finally arriving at Sweeney's bar in Stoneybatter at about ten thirty. There was no sign of Frank.

Timmons entered the pub just after Gerry Thompson, the head barman, had opened the doors. As he went through the doors, the other barman, Liam Connelan, shouted, 'Pint for Mr Timmons?' to which he nodded his head.

'A lovely pint to get you going for the day, Pat,' said Connellan as he placed the still settling pint on Patrick Timmons' table.

'And a small Jemmy as well, Liam,' replied Timmons.

Other morning drinkers came into the bar. He nodded to these, mostly older, men. After two hours of solitary drinking, he borrowed the paper from the counter. The pub was lively and bright and Patrick Timmons liked his local most at this hour of the day.

Momentarily he thought about his children at school and his wife sitting alone at home, smoking in the kitchen. He ordered his sixth pint of the day and a sandwich. He ate and drank and studied the racing form. Frank wasn't coming.

The afternoon drinkers gave way to the evening trade and the bar became noisier and smokier. Timmons watched the clock tick past 5.30 p.m. His co-workers would be finishing work, having completed an honest day's labour Timmons replied labour. By this time he had drunk ten pints and two whiskeys and was talking out loud to himself: 'Why didn't ye show, Frank?'

A crowd of corporation workers came in and one of them greeted him. It was Tom O'Malley, a younger man that he knew from his playing days with the local soccer team. 'Look who we have here boys,' O'Malley shouted sarcastically as he led his friends to the bar, 'the best centre-forward ever to pull on boots for Stoneybatter Celtic!'

'Fuck off,' Timmons replied.

O'Malley was embarrassed in front of his friends and tried to laugh it off. 'Somethin's eatin' yer man, that's for sure,' he said winking over his shoulder at Timmons.

Timmons was annoyed by the arrival of O'Malley and his cronies. His pint tasted sour. He imagined his family at home: the boys finishing their homework and his wife smoking at the kitchen table. He knew they hated his sick days.

Timmons went to the toilet and passed the men at the bar. They made a show of becoming silent as he passed and O'Malley pretended to fix his hair. Timmons' hair was thinning and carefully oiled and combed up from the side.

When he returned to the bar he ordered another whisky and drank it in one mouthful. O'Malley was leaning with his back to the bar with his friends, laughing and joking. Patrick Timmons believed they were laughing at him.

'Yer only a skinny fuck anyway, you never could kick or pass a ball!' he sneered loudly in the direction of O'Malley and his friends.

'Take it easy now, Pat,' cautioned Connelan the barman.

There was no answer from O'Malley or his friends. Then O'Malley said something out of the side of his mouth and all of the men at the bar laughed loudly.

'Didn't you hear me? You fucking mongrel dog, you!' Timmons shouted.

'Knock it off, Timmons,' replied O'Malley warily. His friends began to josh him, sensing the build up to a row.

'You'll have to have it out with him, Tom,' said O'Dwyer, one of O'Malley's friends from the corporation.

'Leave him be, he's pissed,' answered O'Malley.

'I'll piss all over you in a minute,' continued Timmons.

'Are you still talkin' to me, baldy head?'

O'Malley walked to the front of Timmons' table. The bar was silent. For the first time in his life Timmons doubted his strength. He had not felt the familiar and automatic surge of energy catalysed by his anger. O'Malley leaned on Timmons' table with both knuckles down.

'So you'll piss all over me, will you now?' O'Malley said.

'Yeah,' said Timmons through his teeth.

'Right lads,' interrupted Thompson, who would not tolerate fighting inside the pub. 'Outside, not in the bar, please.'

'I'll sort you out now, you skinny fuck,' Timmons said to O'Malley as he lifted himself drunkenly from his seat. His eyes were watery and he felt dizzy and weak. O'Malley and his cronies watched as he staggered to the door and laughed.

Outside the evening air was cold and people passed by on the pavement on their way home from work in the city centre. A few school children skitted around on the pavement outside Kelly's newsagents.

A small circle formed outside Sweeney's pub. Patrick Timmons leaned unsteadily against the pub railings. He wished that he was at home, tired after a hard days' work, eating mashed potatoes, having a laugh with his children and smoking with his wife in the kitchen. He wished he hadn't drunk so much. His rage and anger were gone and had given way to apprehension. Why didn't Frank come, he wondered. Breathing heavily, Timmons put his hand to his chest and could feel the fast, hard beat of his heart as he turned to face O'Malley.

Patrick Timmons lunged at O'Malley, swinging first with his right hand in a wide arcing punch that missed by a distance. Off balance, he swung with his left hand missing also and ending up lying across the front railings of the pub. O'Malley, seeing his chance, gave Timmons a playful kick in the backside, making him look ridiculous. The crowd, which was bigger now, laughed as Timmons pulled his fists in close to his head in the style of a boxer.

'Well if isn't Muhammad Ali!' sneered O'Malley, throwing his first jab catching Patrick Timmons squarely in the face. He confidently flicked out the jab five or six times, scoring easily and setting up the pattern of the fight. In just a few minutes, Timmons was already spent and weakened and could not fight back properly. There was an unfamiliar and overwhelming fear within him, his stomach had turned to water and his legs felt feeble. With all his conviction he wanted to be at home, away from this humiliation.

O'Malley was giving a boxing commentary as he jabbed, hooked and punched Patrick Timmons. 'He ducks, he dives. A lovely jab! What a hook!' O'Malley was full of confidence and was enjoying this opportunity to impress the crowd with his boxing skills. He might as well have been fighting a coat on a coat-stand for all the resistance that Timmons offered. He was drawing blood and punching harder and harder. He continued bludgeoning Timmons.

When the fight was in its final, most humiliating stage, Patrick Timmons' brother-in-law Frank arrived in his work overalls. Through bleeding lips, Timmons mouthed something about the cavalry. He was sprawled against the railings of the pub, his arms lowered and his mouth bloody and torn from the beating. O'Malley was finishing him off with a series of showy hooks and jabs.

'What the fucks goin' on?' Frank shouted as he pushed his way through the crowd and stood between the men.

'Get out of the way 'til I finish that fucker off!' O'Malley shouted as he turned his raised fists to Frank.

O'Malley, confident at having beaten one man, didn't mind taking on a second man. Frank side-stepped the first showy punches and as O'Malley leaned forward, Frank grabbed his hair and pulled his head down to waist level. Swiftly, he delivered five kicks with all of his force to O'Malley's face. He felt the strength leave O'Malley's body and after the fifth kick he knew that he had done enough. The crowd was silent as O'Malley's friends moved to help him to his feet and carried him back into the pub.

'I had him licked. It was only a matter of time before I got him,' Timmons slurred.

Frank led Timmons across the road to the 72 bus stop. People leaning against Mackey's shop window stared at the two men. They waited a few minutes and then Frank changed his mind and led Timmons up Manor Street with the intention of walking home. It took them twenty-five minutes to make the journey and Timmons fell several times on the way up Aughrim Street. The children on the street did not jeer him today. They watched him as he passed, the bloody mess of his face arousing their curiosity, if not their sympathy.

At the top of Oxmantown Road, they turned into Ross Street and saw the 72 bus leave the terminus on its way to Stoneybatter. They rested briefly outside the laundrette at the street corner.

'I'm OK, Frank. Bring me home for the love of God. I need me bed,' Timmons said.

They walked the last hundred yards in silence, finally reaching Patrick Timmons' house.

'She'll have a fit when she sees you like this, Pat.'

'I know, and I have it coming too. I just want to sleep, Frank,' Timmons slurred through swollen lips.

Frank knocked on the door and they waited. Timmons' wife answered the door and stared silently at the two men for a moment.

'I fell by the wayside, Margaret. I fell by the wayside,' Timmons pleaded.

'He's had a hard evening, Margaret. A bit of a ruck,' Frank said.

They came into the sitting room of the house and Frank could see the children peering from behind the bedroom door. It was a sight they had not seen before: their father the ghost, a shuffling, bloody shambles in a coat.

Timmons' wife went to the kitchen and came back with a wet towel. Timmons sat down and allowed her to bathe the cuts and breaks in his flesh. She said nothing at all while she bathed his eyes and cleansed his bloody face. When she was finished she helped him to get out of the dirty, bloodstained coat. Then she went to the kitchen and brought back two plates.

'Ah, you're alright, Margaret, I'm OK,' said Frank with his hand on his stomach.

She ignored him and placed the plates before each of the men. She brought a pot from the kitchen and with a ladle she filled each plate with stew. She said nothing at all to the men and returned to the kitchen.

They smoked another cigarette and then Timmons sat down. He picked up his spoon and tasted the stew his wife had made. His face ached and it hurt when he swallowed. His hands were damaged and were shaking and he could hardly hold the spoon. He put down the spoon and could not eat.

His wife returned from the kitchen and went to the bedroom door where the two boys were peeping out at their father. The children moved from the door and she entered and closed it gently behind her. The men heard some whispering from within and then only silence. When she had the children settled in bed she went back out to the kitchen.

'I give them nothin', Frank. Abolutely nothin', I'm useless to them. My own sons, Frank, seein' their oul' fella beaten up,' Timmons whispered, his voice hoarse.

When Frank finished his stew and his cigarette he put on his jacket. 'You'll be OK in the mornin', Pat, ye always are.' He moved to the door and as he left he said, 'I'll see ye on Saturday, right?'

After Frank left, Timmons tried to finish his stew, which had gone cold. He put down the spoon and pushed back his chair. He wished his children were still awake. He was sorry that he hadn't told his children their story. He stood up and brought his open hands down hard on the table, breaking one of the plates.

'Daddy?' he heard the eldest boy calling from the bedroom. The younger boy began to cry. He could hear his wife moving around in the kitchen.

'Daddy?' he heard again.

'What, love?' he answered.

'Daddy, will you tell us a story tonight?'

'Yes, love, I'll be in now,' he answered. He picked up the broken pieces of the plate from the floor and placed them on the table. He took his cigarettes and matches from his pocket and went into the bedroom he shared with his wife and two sons.

'Tell us about McGuff, Da,' the eldest one whispered from the darkness of the top bunk bed.

Timmons took off his shoes and lay down on the double bed. He took a cigarette, lit it, and inhaled deeply.

'Make a fire ring, Da,' the eldest boy said.

He circled the cigarette in the darkness of the bedroom. Fitfully, he told them the story of McGuff, the man who beat the biggest bully in town. His face hurt and there was an uncomfortable tightness in his chest. After a few minutes the story faltered.

'Are ye alright, Da?'

'Yeah, I'm grand. Grand. Just a little tired that's all.'

'Are ye drunk, Da?' the youngest boy asked.

As he dragged on the cigarette he felt a surge of shame and pain. 'I'm just tired, son, that's all. I'm very tired.' He paused for a moment, inhaled again and said: 'Yes, son, I've had a few drinks. I've had a good few drinks.'

He began the story again. He had lost his way having given in to a compulsion to allow McGuff to lose the fight. He finished two more cigarettes as he struggled to tell the story. On his third cigarette, he yielded to the story and it yielded to his intention. In this double capitulation he found the story's sudden and perfect revelation. From this unconscious harmony, the altered landscape of the story finally surrendered to his imagination. He told it from his heart and it was like no other story he had ever told.

From the bed, he could see through the crack in the door to the room where his wife was sitting. The children were quiet now and the house was perfectly still. When he was finished his final cigarette he waited for a few minutes and then he rose silently from the bed to go and sit with his wife.

He sat at the table and his wife went to the kitchen. She returned with a bowl of hot stew and some fresh bread. She sat beside him and began to feed him. She broke the bread and put it into his mouth and when he was finished each mouthful she gave him a spoonful of the stew. Despite his pain, he savoured its warmth and wholesomeness and he marveled at how fortunate he was to have this good and simple meal. When she was finished feeding him she gently took his damaged and swollen hand, brought it to her lips, and kissed it. For a few minutes they sat and looked at each other saying nothing. One of the children called out to him and he rose and went to the bedroom door.

'Da?' the eldest boy said.

'Yes, son?' he whispered as he leaned into the darkness, his face revealed in the shaft of moonlight that was coming through the small bedroom window.

'That was the best story you ever told us.'

2007

THE GREAT ESCAPE

Michael O'Higgins

Michael O'Higgins worked as a journalist for Hot Press *and* Magill Magazine. *His two stories published in New Irish Writing, 'The Great Escape' (2007) and 'The Migration' (2009) were both Hennessey award-winners. His debut novel will be published by New Island Books later this year. By day, he works as a trial lawyer in the Criminal Courts of Justice. He lives in Bray, County Wicklow with Patricia and his three children.*

I saw his girl Shannon, smiling at the door of the hospital, as soon as we stepped out of the van. The medic hadn't liked the look of Karl, and on the spur of the moment had decided to send him to the Mater for tests. In effect, that meant screening for AIDS and Hepatitis. Karl was only given a few minutes' notice, but it'd been enough to get a message via the bush telegraph. Even though she'd scrambled out of bed, on the back of a text, and was a bit ropey, she was still a bit of a looker.

The jury in the Humphries case was in its third day of deliberations. It was their job to decide whether Joey was the sick bastard who had shot dead a postmistress at point blank range to get his grimy hand on a few thousand euro. Knowing him as I did, I had no doubt. But it was a weak case built around forensics and other circumstantial evidence. The officers doing court escort thought Joey would shade it. The pressure was really getting to him, mind – he was unbearably tetchy and was giving people around him stick. The length of the deliberations had cast a shadow over the whole landing and the tension was making the other prisoners sour.

This was a good day to get off the landing.

As we drew level, she opened her hands, palms up, to show that she wasn't carrying, before casually linking into Karl's free arm. She did this without making any eye contact with me. Close up, her eyes were like little burnt holes in a blanket, her pupils pinpricks, and she was bordering on emaciated, a sure sign that she was using.

She lost no time in giving him a lingering kiss. They both stayed in step. I had no doubt at this very moment her tongue was guiding contraband (most likely hash wrapped in clingfilm) into some recess in his mouth. I jerked Karl's cuffed wrist to indicate my disapproval and pulled up. We resumed our journey, all of us still keeping in step.

'I don't know why he is sending me,' Karl was saying. 'I mean there's spikes going around the landing used by Deco Callaghan but you'd want to have a death wish to share anything used by him.'

'Eric says that you're sure to get the virus.'

'I'll break his fuckin' jaw for him.'

'He says that the place is full of dirty needles.'

'Eric is a fool so he is.'

'When will you get the results?'

'They'll send a letter back to the medical unit.'

There was no test for the virus, only for the antibodies the immune system produced to fight it. If we went back with a fat brown envelope, Karl was fucked – it meant that he was HIV-positive, and the bulk was the standard information pack, explaining how to break the news and arrange for counseling. But it took time for the antibodies to appear. So a skinny missive would only mean that up to three months ago he was not infected. We'd be back again for a follow-up.

With my light-blue shirt and navy trousers I looked like a regular guard in my uniform. Karl, with his wiry frame, Ruud v. Nistlerooy, Man. United top, tracksuit bottoms, and prison pallor, looked like a convict. The Mater was directly across the road from the jail. So you didn't need to be Einstein to work out what the scene was. But if I walked through the concourse with the cuffs visible, everyone would be all eyes. So I draped my jacket over the cuffs in deference to the little bollix. Who says the Irish Prison Service didn't have a little humanity?

I produced the medic's letter of request to the duty nurse. Straightaway she directed us to a cubicle off the beaten track. The hospital didn't like prisoners hanging around any more than we did. Accordingly, every prisoner was automatically triaged as urgent. Karl sat on the examination table with his legs dangling.

After a couple of minutes a young doctor arrived and pulled the curtain over. He asked Karl lots of questions but hardly ever got anything more than a monosyllabic response. Shannon drank coffee from a paper cup and ate a Danish in between texts. I sat on a chair and read my paper.

In the beginning, Shannon had made a big effort to dress up, carefully applied her make up, and with her colour braided hair was very pretty. And in an environment where the predominant colour was battleship grey, very noticeable. Karl strutted imperiously in and out of the visiting boxes proud as. I reckoned that it was this very arrogance that prompted prisoners to break a taboo: they slagged him about what she must be getting up to outside. And, of course, being a punk, it got to him. He gave her a harder time, mind, than the lads winding him up. As if it was all *her* fault for looking good.

I didn't feel much sorry for him, mind. Karl wasn't a difficult prisoner, or anything. Few were when it came right down to it. But he wasn't a nice young lad either. The proof of the pudding was, when he pulled Shannon by the hair around the visiting box, roaring 'slut' – all because when she opened her handbag to get a tissue, he spotted a condom. It was hysterical really, because everyone knew, Karl included, that she was turning tricks on Benburb Street to feed her habit.

After that Karl was put on report. As punishment he was put on screened visits, which meant that he could only see visitors through a glass partition. Nonetheless Shannon meekly followed his instructions to dumb down her appearance. I understood: the last person who had crossed him had got a Heineken bottle smashed into his face. And Karl had gotten five years.

The doctor emerged after a few minutes carrying phials of urine and blood. He signalled by pointing at his watch that he would be back shortly.

Shannon bounded across the floor in a flash. She pulled the curtain across. Between the curtain and the ground I saw her lever off a boot with her heel, and the other soon clanked to the ground beside it. I pictured her standing with her hands on her hips. I heard her climbing up onto the table. Her ankle was the only part of her anatomy visible now. It had a tattoo of a hand holding a rose with a thorny stem dripping a trail of irregularly shaped red drops.

There were murmurs followed almost immediately by a noise like a big dog makes when he is scratching himself behind his ear. But the hospital didn't cater for mangy canines, and anyone coming through the door hearing the din would immediately realise what was going on. I let a roar for them to get on with it.

The beat quickened, more frantic now, rhythmic alright, but still without any melody. There was grunting and the muttering of dirty words on both sides. When Karl eventually let his breath out it sounded like a death rattle. Everything then came to an abrupt silent end.

Shannon hopped onto the floor and slipped on her boots. She hung out of the curtain before blowing him a kiss. On her way out she tossed a tissue into a bin. I saw the pink ring of a condom sticking out of it. I couldn't help thinking that she was probably well used to improvising. She didn't give me a second glance, even though I knew that was an effort.

Karl sat there looking vacant, basking in the afterglow, in the way you do when you have just fucked your woman for the first time in eighteen months. He'd want to tell everyone when he got back, which was a worry.

Karl probably wouldn't see thirty. He didn't own anything. Even the shirt on his back was prison-issue. But he didn't have any debts or responsibilities either. He didn't like Shannon working Benburb Street. But even though she had gone with lots of men, she would never need to look for forgiveness from him. There was something uncomplicated about their relationship that was alluring.

We left with a flat envelope.

I made it clear to him that if he spoke about what had happened we'd see that he did hard time right up to the day of his release. 'Yeah, right,' he'd replied vaguely.

I was drinking a cup of tea in the canteen when the ACO directed me to go to the Governor's office immediately. I didn't like that he didn't say much on the way over.

The Governor was sitting at his desk. He pointed me to sit down. The Assistant Governor and Personnel Manager were standing alongside him, all business. At least there was no one from the Prison Officers' Association.

'How did the hospital go?'

'Fine.'

'Anything,' and he paused, 'anything unusual happen?'

The antennae were up. But their faces were inscrutable. CCTV? It was everywhere. But I knew there was no way the hospital could tolerate it in a cubicle where intimate examinations took place.

'No,' I replied.

'So, is that what I will tell the Security Corrs from *The Irish Times* and the *Star* when they ring back?' The very casual way he said it was designed to put me off my stride.

'I guess.' I stayed non-committal.

But I was in the shit. Why else would the papers be looking for him to comment? Had Shannon passed something really awful in that kiss?

'I dare say Charlie Bird will on by lunchtime,' he added.

I stayed *stom.*

The Governor gestured for me to come around to his side of his desk. He pointed at his desktop.

'See do you recognise anyone?'

The video was captioned: 'Joy of Sex is nothing to Sex in the Joy'. Since it had been uploaded at 11.48 a.m., it had already been viewed 32,987 times, thirteen of them on this very terminal. I wondered what they had been saying when they watched it the previous twelve times.

I watched Shannon straddling Karl. It was an overhead shot. The quality was surprisingly good considering Shannon was multitasking. If you looked really close you could see a pair of shoes under the curtain. They could enhance that. I made a note to get rid of the shoes I was wearing.

'How do you suppose this happened?'

I shrugged. Blackberrys were the hottest contraband these days. Shannon, the little wagon, had filmed it, and then, no doubt, shared it about. It didn't take long for someone to get the bright idea of uploading the images onto YouTube.

We watched in silence. Just before they reached the point of no return, I heard a muffled bellow: 'Hurry the fuck up will you?'

'Who is speaking there do you think?' the Governor asked.

'No idea, what is it exactly?'

'It's perfectly obvious what it is. The prisoner is having sexual intercourse with a female on your watch.' The way he said *fee-male* made him sound like Special Branch.

'Well. I didn't see any of that,' I said with just the right level of indignation of someone telling the literal truth.

'And how is it that you didn't see it?'

'Maybe I went to the loo?' I knew that was a lame excuse, but if I admitted that I had facilitated them I was history.

'The footage lasts over three minutes. Long time to be at the toilet.'

I didn't reply.

'What do you suppose I tell the papers? That you were in the toilet wiping your arse? I am suspending you with immediate effect. There will be a disciplinary hearing before the end of the week. Get yourself a good brief.'

I was relieved that prisoners were on lock up as I crossed D Landing. I heard loud screeching, prisoners swearing in jubilation and banging the pipes in their cell. It came out of nowhere. For a brief moment I thought it was for my benefit. But such a cacophony could only mean one thing: Joey Humphries had been acquitted.

People assume that criminals are hard and uncaring, but in my experience, most have a streak of decency too. They weren't whooping it up for Joey. Humphries was a bully who couldn't even do his time. They saw his crime for the act of cowardice it was.

For years, I had watched judges direct verdicts of not guilty, on technicalities. But prisoners saw judges, courts and lawyers as cogs in a bigger wheel, which ground them to dust. That was why Shannon had never acknowledged me. It was nothing personal. The Governor's description of sex with a female, when he well knew it was Shannon, was the same mindset. They cheered alright, but only for a victory over a system they hated.

I could already see the headlines in tomorrow's papers: 'SCREW KEEPS NICKS WHILE INMATE HAS SEX IN A&E'. There'd be questions asked in the Dáil. I could drag it out for a year or two through the appeals and the courts all on full pay. And then resign just before all the manoeuvres were exhausted. It all seemed futile.

I gathered up my bits and pieces from my locker, ancient pictures of the kids pinned to the door, bits of paper with notes scrawled upon them that made no sense now, newsletters, disposable razors, toiletries and other detritus. I binned everything except the pics even though the faded colours had drained them of vitality.

For twenty years I'd been a turnkey. I had cut down the sheets from which five prisoners (Fleming, Walsh, Kinch, Fahy and Williams (Anita), had hung, and seen others turned blue, choked on their own vomit. Fahy had thrown boiling water laced with sugar over me long before he'd topped himself. My back was badly scarred.

I'd near shit myself the first time I'd walked the landings. It didn't take long to learn to swagger. It took a lot longer to realise I was doing a job, the prisoners were doing their time, and that we were all in this together. I hadn't borne any grudges.

I walked across the yard to the front gate. The word was out. Officers were averting my gaze. I didn't care. I was never coming back here. I felt elated, like a prisoner must feel when an appeal court unexpectedly quashes his conviction and he is free to go. Maybe later I would feel differently. But, I didn't think so. My mind was made up. This was for keeps.

MUSCLE MEMORY

Nicola Jennings

Nicola Jennings was the Deirdre Purcell Short Story competition winner in 1999 and the Maria Edgeworth Short Story winner in 2000. She has also been a contributor to Sunday Miscellany *on* *RTÉ Radio 1. Since 'Muscle Memory' was shortlisted for a Hennessy Award, her collection of stories,* Horse *made the final in the 2012 Eludia Awards in Philadelphia.*

For whatever we lose (like a you or a me)
it's always ourselves we find in the sea.

e. e. cummings

She was in the sea, supported by the water that surrounded her. Floating, she was of the water and part of the water. It took away her woes and cares, her pains and aches, the stiffness of her joints, the heaviness of her years. That was the plan and it was working. The water eased her confusion, lightened her depression and calmed her mind. Here no one could reach her to question her or organise her. Here she was free. She knew that dead men's bones littered the seabed far beneath her. Dead men's fingers rippled among the tendrils of seaweed floating and swirling around the rocks. On the horizon black storm clouds were harbingers of death. Oh she knew, knew it all. Knew why she was here, rocking in the sea. She knew where she was, even who she was, but how had she got here? She couldn't remember that. And what was the plan? Already she had forgotten. Perhaps, if she concentrated hard enough, memory would come back to her. It did that sometimes. Lucidity in a flash. Clarity when she least expected it. Surprising her with awareness, understanding, memories, and always fear. Perhaps she wasn't alone, here, in the dark water. Perhaps they were watching her now. Waiting for her to make a mistake, forget something, put a foot wrong. She squinted around her into the bright sunlight, but could see no one. The shore looked very distant, just a thin line of grey, another of green, the blue shadowy mountains behind. Above them the clouds looked even more menacing than they had only a moment before.

She moved her right leg carelessly, experimentally, lifted it and watched the water stream back from it into the sea where it belonged. Lifted the other. Repeated the process. She could still swim. Swim well. So many other things were lost to her now, but she hadn't forgotten that. She swayed and swayed with the rocking sea, floating on her back, her eyes closed against the bright sky above her, savouring freedom. Then she shivered as the sky darkened. The sun was being obscured by dark clouds. She could see that through her closed eyelids and could feel the coolness on her skin. She turned and swam, strongly, just as before. Swimming was always her delight, her escape and her joy. It held so many connections with her past, her missing fragmented past. It was while swimming, powering through the blue pool early on a Sunday morning, that she first met him. She couldn't remember his name, could hardly remember his face, but she knew he had been important to her once. Pet, he called her, or was it sweetheart? Perhaps she loved him. Were they lovers? Were they married? Were there children somewhere, anxious to be recognised, acknowledged, grieving her absence yet presence, her inbetweenness – neither one thing nor the other. She tried to drag his likeness before her, but all she could manage was the touch of his hand on her skin, her skin rippling with delight and pleasure, the strength of his fingers as he pinched her flesh between his finger and thumb, near pain and yet not pain, and his eyes laughing at her. Or was it just the water washing her, breaking against her, sparkling around her? There was nothing else in her mind. Just a gaping blank.

And where was she now? Why was she here? Was there a plan? If there was it was lost. For a moment she forgot her surroundings, content in the brief tenuous luxury of a memory, however fragile, however incomplete. Unaware that in that one precious absorbing moment her body, heavy and weary, had begun to drag her down. The bones below were calling to her bones, a seductive siren song, luring them to the bottom of the sea. Down there, bones were ground by the swell and drag of the waves into tiny grains of sand just like all the other grains. Pretty, not bone anymore, but different shades of stone and shell and silica. Indistinguishable from each other. Fine and running finely like the sand in the egg timer in the kitchen, her blue and white kitchen, the sands of time and the end of everything.

Her clothes were heavy and sodden about her, weighing her down. Only her shoes were missing. But why was she wearing her clothes, why was she fully dressed here in the sea, far out from the beach? Was that part of the plan? Everything it seemed was conspiring to take her and place her where she belonged among the sleek and silvery sinuous fish, their unblinking eyes watching her, their mouths gaping, ravenous, would be scavengers of her flesh. The crabs too would have their share. Rich pickings, fine food for crustaceans, a fair repayment for all the crab salads and lobster bisque she had eaten in her lifetime. She could still remember food. She could remember the taste and smell and texture of food. Even as she drifted and sank, drifted and sank, washed around by the currents, even as her face felt water cold against it, and her hair splayed out behind her, even as the skin on her fingers was grey and crumpled and wrinkled by the long immersion in salt water, even still she could remember meals in fine restaurants, his arms resting on the tabletop as he wooed her, charmed her, but she could not remember his name, only her longing for him. Only the weeping and the longing. And her mother. She too she could only make out dimly in her mind – remembering the hot meals at the kitchen table, the blue and white kitchen, the Christmas dinners and the birthday teas. Lost in the shadows were the people who had been there then, what they wore, what they said and whether they might have loved her once.

She couldn't recall yesterday or last week, or remember appointments, or unpaid bills, couldn't take the car anymore up the mountains, away from the city and lie in the long grass with him, the white clouds scudding across the blue sky above, tiny spiders spinning webs in the heather. She tried again but she still couldn't remember his name, his face, or his voice but the watch he wore on his wrist and the worn brown leather strap, oh that came clearly to mind well enough. The time passing on the white dial with the silver numbers, until all the time passed, all her allotted time, that she remembered, and she was here now, in the sea, with her grief and her confusion and her plan and the waves were more choppy and the water wilder. She turned back to look at the beach, still a distant line, where she thought she could see figures, movement, colours, but she wasn't sure. She wasn't sure where she was any more either, or why, and her face was wet and she could taste the salt of her tears on her lips, or was it sea salt? Fear gripped her. She panicked and struggled and forgot how to move her arms and her legs. She was cold and deathly tired and the sea anemones far below were waving their tentacles in the tide as though they were welcoming her. Beside her a jellyfish rocked and floated and touched her gently. She looked at it for a long time in wonder, knowing there was something about this soft, almost invisible thing. Finally remembering the sting and the pain on the beach, someone pouring milk on the sting and wrapping her in a red and yellow towel on a pebbly beach and cold ham, and salad, and white sliced pan, and then nothing? Her thoughts were coming faster and faster, and more and more jumbled, and she was sinking. Hands were reaching up from the bottom of the sea, dead men's hands, reaching up to claim her, to unite her with the lost and the confused, the desired and the forgotten. And hands were reaching down from above, raising her up and bringing her back, lifting her dripping out of the water and into a boat but why? And faces were gazing at her, alarmed, anxious, curious faces. Then she was on the beach and wrapped again in a red and yellow towel but why? And voices were calling her 'Mother!' and 'Nan!' Faces, completely unknown to her, strangers, were hugging her and kissing her and saying 'Thank God you're all right' 'Such a fright.' And 'What on earth happened?' And indeed what on earth had happened?

She felt very small, insignificant and lost and alone, surrounded by people who seemed to think they knew her better than she did herself, who seemed to know she liked hot sweet tea and wore navy and parted her hair on the right. And where was he? Why hadn't he come to rescue her? She thought she remembered his name then, spoke it in a low clear small voice,

'Dad?'

Saw their faces drop, their exchange of looks, and thought – that's wrong. I've got it wrong. Joe, or Tony, or George? Nothing seemed right. Reminded herself not to say anything out loud ever again unless she was absolutely sure she had it right – she didn't want to see consternation on anyone's face ever again. Wouldn't speak. No. Not ever again. There would be silence, and then there would be oblivion. The little crabs would scurry over her eyelids and between her fingers and she would not know. Everything would finally be forgotten. No one would remember how she loved him and how he left her, how she wept and how it was all absolutely over now. Over and over again. Over.

2008

DROWN TOWN

Colm Keegan

Colm Keegan has been shortlisted twice for the Hennessy Awards with his stories, and twice with his poems. His poetry collection, Don't Go There, *was released in 2012. He is a founding member of Lingo, Ireland's first spoken-word festival, and is currently Writer in Residence for DLR LexIcon.*

I've never felt more alive.

A big bass beat is thumping through the ground and into me from what might be the night's last song. The whole place is kicking, I'm drugged up and flying. My heart is going wild, buzzing off the energy of all the people as I cross the dance floor. I'm with my mate Darin and he's flying too, sure I can nearly see his wings. Coolness comes off us like a Ready-Brek glow. It's in our eyes, in my gelled hair, in the Ronnie Darin's trying to grow, and in our movement, the way we walk, half-dancing.

Darin points and shouts over the music.

'Let's go over there.'

I follow him up into the tiered seating. The air smells of grass. People have flipped down the blue plastic seats to stand on and dance. We get up as well and give it loads; our arms flying, legs not moving, wearing our best ravers' faces and gurning to fuck. The song changes and a piano solo fills the air. I turn my face upwards and let the music pour over me, getting lost in the one taps me on the shoulder. A dancer on the ...ves a spliff in my face. I give a thumbs-up and ...ag of the joint. The smoke tickles my brain. I check out the dance floor, a lake of bodies washed in laser green. I try to give the joint back but its giver closes his eyes and shakes his head back into the beat. I call to Darin.

'D'ya want this?' I wave the spliff and he takes it, but hands it back with a wink after one quick toke.

'We have to get down there,' I say. 'Get back into it.'

He does an OK sign with his hand and his grin widens. He hasn't got a clue what I'm saying, but it stops mattering. The joint has me gone all ripply.

I close my eyes and rise with the music, I see myself skimming along the Liffey, bridges rushing over me. I spiral up and around Liberty Hall and skip onto the top of the Custom House, seeing orange light streaking through the river like rocket trails from the buildings, or stilts keeping everything afloat.

Darin tugs at my T-shirt.

'You alright?'

'Yeah man, I'm sound.' He's all blurry, like he's behind dirty glass.

'We're gonna do it tonight,' he says. 'Arnott's, right?'

'Yeah, I'd say so, yeah.'

He's on about our deal. A promise we made ourselves one night on Henry Street.

'We have to. We will,' he's trying to convince himself.

'There's no panic,' I say again. 'We'll see what happens.'

I spot a perfect candidate for the spliff. A girl about my age in a purple lace dress that clings to everything walks by on the dance floor, the lights pick out glitter on her tights, ultraviolet makes her trainers gleam and little freckles stand out on her cheeks. She stops and grabs a handrail and totters a bit, she's gorgeous and she's out of it. I jump down off the chair and trot down to her in time to the beat. But then I can't think of anything to say. I just stand there with the music bashing my ears.

A big thick with his collar popped up comes over and grabs her by the waist, swings her around and tries to kiss her. She's having none of it but she doesn't squirm out of his grip either. I go over and offer him the joint.

'What the fuck is that?' he says, staring at the joint as if I've just flashed him.

'It's a J. Wanna toke, bud?'

'I'm not your bud, prick.' A frown tightens his big, spotty, angry head. I'd say in the daylight the hairs on his knuckles cast shadows. I can tell he would like to smash my face in, he's the type that would do it out of boredom. That's why I have a Stanley blade tucked into my sock, not that I'd ever cut anybody, but I bring it just in case. Everyone carries something.

'No bother, man,' I say. 'It's cool, more for me.' I take a big pull on the joint.

He moves away and tries to pull her with him into the crowd. She looks my way and stays still, their fingers play for a second, then he's floating alone. He reaches into his top and swigs from a bottle of vodka before turning away with a grumble. She gives a little trickly wave and laughs.

'Bye-Bye, Vodka Boy.'

The girl wobbles again so I stamp out the joint and offer help. She drops into my arms, her head falls back, her hair goes across her face in strands but I can still see her eyes, the nicest I've ever seen. The DJ weaves classical music into the sounds.

'Hello there,' I say.

'Hello yourself,' she says.

Around us everybody is drowning in the swirl of violins, eyes closed, arms up, bodies swaying. I hold the girl's hips from behind and pull her body against mine. My little finger slides up her tights. We lean backwards together, arching our backs to send rushes up our spines. The beat builds up, the crowd moves quicker now. I let my lips get close to her ear, my chin feels the sweat on her neck. The floor starts shaking as the beat kills off the violins. The whole place jumps up and down. A roar swells up from the crowd. We separate and join the motion. I throw out a few two-fingered whistles. My buzz spills out onto my face in a big yoked-up smile. Everything is lovely, we're all moving together with the beat and I've never felt more alive.

The song stops. The lights go on. It's all over. I turn to grab her and kiss her but she's gone. I tell myself it's all good but the vibe is changing, something mean snakes through the place, infecting my belly. The magic is lost, it's all skaggy faces and people shouldering for space.

That time on Henry Street; me and Darin were on mushrooms, trippin to bits, sharing his iPod and painting pictures with the tunes. It was sunny after raining and the streets were all glimmery. Outside Arnott's there was this homeless man warming a strip of cardboard, a smelly drunk fucker, all beardy and piss-stained with only cider cans for company. He waved us over. We just smirked and kept walking, but he got up and grabbed us, started screaming into our faces. Darin couldn't handle it and just broke his shite laughing. I laughed as well. Then the man gave me a full force clatter in the face. I stood holding my cheek, pure silent as my buzz went all bogey. The tramp's gummy, reeking mouth became a black hole sucking me in. Darin saw me slipping, grabbed my shoulders and pointed up at the sky.

'We should dance up there!' he said.

'What?' I looked up, big, tripped eyes blinking.

'Up there.' He was pointing at the top of Arnott's. 'Next week after the rave.'

When I realised what he was at I started laughing again, rescued.

'Yeah! That'd be fucking legend man.'

We walked off, talking real loud to let the dipso know he hadn't hurt us. He didn't know what was going on. We huddled close together over our new plan. All the way back to the flats we talked ourselves onto the buildings, imagining our arms in the air like the statues on O'Connell Street, but with headphones on, sparkling like the Spire, dancing over the empty streets as they swirled around us.

Some sap slips on the dancefloor and stumbles into me. I push back and we stare at each other. There's a shout from up in the chairs. Bouncers have a hold of the dancer that gave me the spliff. Vodka Boy is there as well, smirking. Darin's in the middle of it, his body language pleading to the listening bouncers. Whatever happened is done with until Spliffy loses it and starts swinging digs. I get up to Darin just as he side-steps the scrap, smart enough not to get sucked in. But that Vodka muppet pushes the two of us flying. We lash into a bouncer and then everything takes off.

Vodka's laughing with a big spiteful grin on his face, crooked teeth showing in his half-cocked mouth. Darin manages to go for him. Vodka's buddy jumps on Darin, then I'm on the deck from a punch, getting kicked. I crawl clear. The whole tier is in uproar. People are falling off and over the chairs. Vodka's lashing Darin's head off the ground. I reach for the Stanley blade and give Vodka a boot that catches him lovely and then I slice at his face, missing on purpose. He backs off. Darin gets loose. Someone shouts about the knife. Space opens up around me and I'm free until the bouncers are on us again, bending our arms behind our backs and grabbing our hair. The knife disappears.

We're thrown out one of the emergency exits, let loose on the summer night. There must be about twenty of us but I don't know who's with who. Vodka appears in front of me and bashes his naggin into my head. The glass smashing makes me think of cash registers. My tooth chips, but I hardly feel it. Then it's blast off again, we're all punching and kicking, moving in circles. Everybody's night is ruined now, somebody is going to pay.

There's a fence of bouncers blocking people from joining in but some get through. We jostle out of the car park towards the Liffey. I touch my bleeding head and feel only a tiny little cut. We spill out onto the road. Outsiders get swallowed by the madness, trying to help or getting smart and getting attacked for getting too near.

The rave pours out more and more spectators, yelling and whistling, clapping even. I see the girl from the dance floor with a gang of women high on the drama. Some are baring their teeth, nearly shouting at the sky. But she is still gorgeous though.

Darin runs from my side into the middle of the road shouting. He bounces through the mob, lashing at anyone in reach. Everything moves away from him like ripples from a stone. His top is all torn so he rips it off, his body is slick, the tendons stick out on his neck, for a second he's got control as if he owns the whole street. Then someone sees their chance and knocks him flying with a box. Everybody starts running.

A faux-hawked poser jumps at me and I level him with one punch. We zigzag through the traffic lights near the Custom House, the roads throb under our galloping feet, everything's tense. People are roaring and barking – deep round sounds that start in their ribcages. It's like the most you should ever want to do is scream. A car drives past, kicks batter its flanks, something smashes through the windscreen. The hairs prickle up on my neck. I've never felt more alive.

A raver in combats stands on the granite wall of the Liffey, lets out this huge fucking roar as people throng the edge of the swollen river. Whether he falls or jumps or gets pushed in I don't know. But someone else goes after him, then another and another. Darin has someone in a headlock and is trying to force him over the wall, he grabs the belt of his enemy's jeans and manages to flip him in only for his neck to get grabbed. So he goes in as well. It's all yells and splashes as people enter the flow.

There's about fifty people treading water now in the river, laughing and calling others to leave the street behind. Fellas acrobat through the air. Girls hand their things to friends and take the plunge in their minis and bras. People line the walls of the river clapping and cheering. I hear a young one's voice and see my girl leaning over the edge. Now's the time to catch her and kiss her, but she climbs up and waves at me before jumping in with a splash.

Two shit-vans turn up, painting everything blue and making people scatter. I run for the wall. A girl garda grabs for me but I dodge her and dive in head first.

The wind flies through my hair and then there are bubbles in my ears. I swim under the surface. I used to dream of playing in the Liffey when I was small. Football or kiss-chasing under Tara Street Bridge. Loads of little eight-year-olds on water like glass. The cold brings my buzz back and it shoots through me in tingles. I stretch and float, wiggling my toes in my runners.

I swim around the edge of the crowd. The river is warm, the noise of it tickles my ears, the way it slides off my arms when I raise them from the water. Darin starts singing some song at the top of his voice, all the swimmers join in and so do I. A few of the police start laughing. I see my girl treading water over near the far wall. She waves again. Then I hear movement in the water behind me and it's Vodka with his face all stiff and he sort off hugs me hard and I feel something stick into my side. The pain of it gets me jumping and twisting like a fish on a line.

I manage one big shout and then I feel all dopey. Darin gets over to me and he can't tell what's wrong. My mouth won't work and I know that it's shock, and my hands are tight on my side and underwater Darin feels my stomach spilling into the river.

He shouts for help but nobody's listening, everybody's still having fun. Vodka's over at one of the ladders crawling up and out of the water. The Liffey is in my eyes and tears are coming out, everything's gotten nicer because I think I might be dying, all the streetlights are blurry and look like orange stars.

My girl comes over to help and I want to kiss her. Because I might sink and never come up if it wasn't for her, if it wasn't for the care in her eyes. I look above at all the people, at nobody giving a fuck and Darin screams so loud it's like his throat is tearing as the sound flies over the river.

The whole city turns to look at us. I'll never feel more alive.

AMONG THE LIVING

Selina Guinness

Selina Guinness lectures in English literature at IADT Dun Laoghaire and farms in the Dublin Mountains. 'Among the Living' (2009) was her first published story. In 2012, Penguin Ireland published her memoir, The Crocodile by the Door, *which was shortlisted for the Costa Book Awards and the Bord Gáis Energy Irish Book Awards, 2012. Her short story, '*The Weather Project*', appears in* All Over Ireland, *edited by Deirdre Madden and published by Faber & Faber in 2015.*

It was the tiniest lamb he had yet to deliver. Inside the ewe, its head felt so small, he thought it was a foot. His face twisted as the sharp pelvic bones grinded against his hand. He gasped at his wife to keep the ewe quiet so he could find the two front legs to draw the lamb. He was up to his armpit now, and in all the tight vastness, he couldn't work it out – was that a leg, or a head? He passed his fingers over the obstacle and curled them around what seemed to be a neck; very small. There, tucked behind, that was a knee, and moving back up to the shoulders, he found the other foreleg. Fine now; he had the two hooves in his fist. He pulled, and the hooves came forwards and appeared in the stable dark, black, the same size as the dags in her tail, and then in one swift slither, the lamb was out, still wrapped in its sac. 'Aborted,' he told his wife, but when he rubbed the weak body with his gloved hand, he felt a convulsion. 'No, it's still alive,' he told her. She could hear the suppressed satisfaction in his voice. He cleared the mucus from its nostrils before sliding the lamb under the nose of its mother, who rumbled and started to lick it clean. They both stood back then. Her first lamb was already up on his staggery legs, hunched, but of a good size – though not enormous, so you could not say he had taken from his twin.

There was no chance of it suckling so they brought it up to the kitchen. He fetched a hot water bottle, wrapped it in cloths and covered it with straw in a cardboard banana box before gently lifting the lamb on top for her to towel off the fluids and allay its shivering. 'Its body is scarcely the span of my hand,' she declared, her voice soft, as he fetched out the Pyrex jug from the press.

Under the bare bulb in the scullery, he measured out three scoops of powdered colostrum from a small plastic tub and filled up the jug with warm water. The stomach tube needed cleaning. The syringe had fallen under the sink among the gumboots. He retrieved it, and gave it a shake. 'I'll need a hand,' he said, and so she lifted the box into the boiler room and together they squatted down, slapping aside the damp laundry, to attend to feeding it.

Gripping the jaw in his right hand, he used his index finger to press down the tongue and, with his left, he took the tube from her. He passed the clear end smoothly over his forefinger and down its throat, trying to keep the tube as close to the roof of its mouth as possible. When just three inches remained, he licked his top lip and bent down to press the protruding end against it to check for a whisper of air. 'I think it's all right,' he said, lifting his head, and she filled the syringe up to the fifty ml mark. He took it from her and fixed on the plastic nozzle.

She would not watch. The previous week she had come down in the middle of the night to feed a lamb with hypothermia, and despite having done all her husband was doing now, and with the greatest of care, she had passed the tube not into the lamb's stomach, but down its windpipe. Cradled on her lap, it had coughed and struggled a little as the milk went down before closing its eyes as the milk filled up its lungs until a thin stream poured back out its nose, spilling onto her thigh through her apron. Back in bed, she had lain awake, struggling to convince herself that drowning in a mother's milk must be the kindest way to go.

The lamb's eyes opened as the colostrum inflated its sides, as if it were attached to a bicycle pump. Her husband withdrew the tube, shook off the drips onto the straw and got to his feet. 'We'll see. It'll be a miracle if it survives the night.'

They went to bed. 'Solicitous, that's what he is,' she thought, and her mind travelled back to a seminar she had attended at college. They had been discussing the marriage of Gabriel and Gretta Conroy in 'The Dead'. 'Solicitude is no substitute for passion,' the lecturer had said. But even then she had felt he was wrong. In the battle of the angels, it had been Gabriel's concern for her that drew Gretta towards him along that shaft of light. How close she had kept the flare of Michael Furey's passion but what did it really signal that a man had died for her? She'd been snagged by his memory on the stairs, and left ragged like a strand of wool on barbed wire. And she was sure that Gabriel already knew, if not the story, then the force of his wife's remembered passion, for he was stirred by it, and perhaps because he was stirred, he had not sought to pry. If only he had had the sense, he could have seen it as a flare from a boat and swum out to it: an annunciation, perhaps, or the chance of new life.

Her feet were cold. She turned towards her husband, and curled into the question mark of his body, warming the tops of her feet against his soles. 'I don't like dogs,' he had told her on their first walk together. 'You mean you're scared of them,' she had teased. 'No, I don't like what dogs do to people. No animal should be made a pet, it's demeaning.' 'Demeaning of the animals, or their owners?' she'd asked. 'The humans,' he'd replied. And since they had started farming he had held true to this, for he showed no sentimentality in his care of the flock. Without wincing, he could turn a ewe on her backside and cut deep between her hooves to excavate foot rot, and when the black lamb was born with its joints fused so it could not stand, the next morning he had taken it away. 'Do you really want to know?' he had asked with clear distaste, before giving the plain answer: 'With a blow of the sledge hammer to its head.'

That was like him. He flinched from nothing. From the first, she'd felt he could hold her up to the light and read not just what she had written there to be read, but the half-formed letters between the lines, all her hesitations. Of course this meant too that he could trace the shape of Nathan like a watermark on her character. It had taken one long car journey early on to tell him the story, and he had remained quiet for most of it. 'If he walked in to your life now, what would you do?' he had asked eventually. 'I don't know,' she had replied, 'I couldn't honestly say I wouldn't walk back out with him,' she paused, 'but I don't know whether the lack of him has come to mean more.' She watched him as he drove on, his Adam's apple bobbing up and down as he struggled to control his hurt. And as the motorway took them north, she began to recognise that in the light of his struggle towards generosity seen in his grim concentration on the road ahead, her own answer was pitiful. It was nothing but a sentimental attachment to her own exoticism that kept her clinging to this past affair.

He felt more solid here under her arm; work on the farm had thickened his chest and shoulders. Although he said he was getting old, he was, she felt, getting stronger. She let her lips graze the soft stubble at the back of his neck. 'Always warm,' was her last thought before sleep, 'he's always warm.'

It was surprising how confident he had become at the farming. Once more he listened for the lamb's breath at the end of the tube, and hearing nothing, pressed down the plunger on the syringe. He had expected to find it dead this morning, but the little thing had survived the night. He retracted the tube, and put his hand on her tiny ribcage to feel the heart hammering away. As he stood up, her body convulsed a little and a small gobbet of milk flew out of her mouth. It was only the prelude. He felt his spirits sinking as he watched her over the next few minutes throw up the entirety of what he'd fed her. So, she has problems with her digestive system, he thought, that would explain her size. Maybe if he diluted down the next feed and gave her less she'd take it. He searched around for a rag with which to pick up the soiled straw and put it in a plastic bag.

It was the challenge of farming, he'd explained to his wife, that he enjoyed. Not many men at the age of forty got the chance to do something completely different with their lives, and fewer still found they could put their family at the centre of it. This time his most strenuous endeavours would be claimed not by books but by living duties and affections. He sat at the kitchen table and drank his coffee. It was perhaps a more profound revelation than he had then realised. He had meant her of course, and their son, but he had other duties too. The decision of his teenage daughter, Anna, to leave her mother and come live with them had offered him the unexpected chance to redeem his younger self. The memory of his first marriage still stung him. He had known himself so little then, and the fact that children were born out of his confusion and had to suffer the consequences of the inevitable breakdown, still filled him with shame. He rose quickly and cleared his cup and plate away, and went to the back door to put on his oilskins, cap and boots. The bundle of heavy keys was hanging on a hook, the largest for the old stables where the rest of the orphaned lambs were. He picked up the feed bucket from outside the door, with the bottles he'd made earlier still warm inside, and headed out, thinking on what he would do.

Down in the yard, the ewe from last night was letting her first lamb feed, turning to sniff his tail occasionally to check he was her own. He filled up a bucket with water and poured more nuts into the feeding trough and then watched them for a moment. They had not had much success with fostering, but maybe this ewe would work, for the little one in the boiler room would not be returning to her. He climbed into the pen and caught her as she bolted. With his knee, he wedged her up against the wall and reached down to check her spins. A ready spurt of milk came from each one. She had plenty of milk to spare.

He walked back to the house. He could hear music from Anna's room, and he smiled as he recognised the song she had been listening to over and again every morning these past few months. His wife was not yet up – she would bring Sam down soon. He went into the boiler room and lifted the tiny lamb out of its box. He hoped it still bore enough of its mother's fluids for this to work.

At the back door, he got to work on the lamb he'd selected from among the pen of orphans. It too had been born in the last twenty-four hours, and was on the small side, so with any luck the ewe would take the stranger for her own. The first thing was to get it wet and steaming with water from the kettle. Then he took up the tiny lamb, and rubbed its limp body over the orphan's forequarters and head to transfer the scent. The action seemed to warm life into both of them; the tiny one stirred in his hand and bleated for the first time. It was hardly a cry.

A tap on the window pane made him turn around. His wife was standing there with their son in her arms, watching him. She opened the door. 'Do you think it will work?' she asked. 'I don't know,' he said, 'but there's more chance with this one's mother than there has been with any other.' 'And how's Tiny doing?' she nodded at his hand. 'I don't think it will live,' he said. 'Here,' putting Sam down, she stepped out onto the concrete in her bare feet, 'pass her over. If you're going back down to the yard with him, I'll try and give this one another feed.' She listened as he instructed her to dilute the milk down and give a half measure. 'OK?' he asked, and she understood that he meant more than whether she now knew what she had to do. 'Yes, fine.' She nodded. He picked up the stronger lamb by his two front legs and moved to go, but she stopped him and said lightly, 'When we first met, did either of us ever imagine we'd be here, doing this together?' Behind her, Sam had picked up the stomach tube and was whacking a gumboot with it. Although she had meant it lightly, the question seemed to resonate in the cold morning air. He stood there with his foot on the first step, the orphan's head lolling against his leg, and his eyes searched her face as they used to do when first they lay together. She held the tiny lamb closer against her dressing gown, and only dared to breathe herself, when finally she heard him give the answer that would, she felt, suffice her for a long time yet: 'No, but can you imagine now living any other way?'

2009

STEPS OF STAIRS

Niamh Boyce

Niamh Boyce won the Hennessy New Writer of the Year Award for her poem 'Kitty'. Her novel, The Herbalist, *won Newcomer of the Year at the 2013 Irish Book Awards and was longlisted for the IMPAC Award. Her poetry collection was highly commended in the 2013 Patrick Kavanagh Award. She is currently working on a new novel.*

The look he stole ran the morning cold. The scissors became a dead weight in my hand. Their chat went on but I didn't hear any of it. Wrong was being done. I knew. I just knew. Like Mother did. Aren't you a real daddy's girl? she'd taunt. And somewhere between that sentence and her unsmiling eyes, it was written. The way a bitter day shows up your breath.

She never touched me, our mother. Held me in contempt, is all. Why? That's a road I can't go down. A graveyard tells you nothing with its tongues of stone. As long as the little lad was all right. The apple of her eye. That's what I thought, that she'd draw the line if it was him. Girls counted for nothing in our house. Steps of stairs, people called us. Me, Sis and Ben.

And we were.

One day I found Ben in the shed. His arms wrapped around his legs, a wet cheek to his knee. It was where I went too, to sit small on empty coal bags. The plastic roof was the colour of flypaper and outside the lilac would creak against the sunlight, its branches looming and tapping as leaf shadows played over and over on my skin. Magic things lie in the jammed drawers of that soggy old dresser, you know, I whispered to Ben, treasure maps, belonging to deadly pirates. He became my first mate. I held him and told him stories. He was only a whip of brown eyes and puppy fat. The democracy of the cruelty made it insurmountable. More the way things are, and always will be, Amen.

Thank God for his work. It kept him, tired him. *A working man I am.* He'd soap his arms to the elbows, leave tide marks on the yellow basin. Why did it take so long to be free? Ben's teacher calling to the house was the beginning, though we didn't know it then. Mother's shoulders were the first part of her to surrender. She became careless. The forgotten iron smoked round-bottomed triangles onto our sheets. The burnt pattern of her shame enshrouded our sleep. She lost her glasses, her keys … even gave up her daily warnings. I let Breda into our kitchen for a glass of water and she didn't bat an eyelid. She stopped looking both ways when she crossed. Eventually, she ended up dead on the road. Like a stray. The car skidded to a stop, some seconds too late. I'm unkind? Yes. No forgiveness there. I hate her more than him. Yet I bawled when we buried her. Wished I could wrap myself alongside her, to see if she were as soft as I had once imagined she might be.

He'd be drunk. Every saint known to man surveyed us and stayed silent in their ceramic gazes. *Saint Martin, help me.* He was choking slowly to death on coal dust. An industrial disease. Died within a year of her. People thought it was hard on us. Orphaned. I didn't have his name inscribed under hers on the headstone. I won't be paying for that any day soon. I've paid. Those who know where he's buried won't need reminding. Those who don't, are better off not knowing.

Not knowing. That's what Mother said. About sex, though she never used the word. God forbid. It was when Aunt Esther died. As wizened, and as pure, as the day she was born. *It's better to die like Esther, to die not knowing.* She sounded envious. We lived in a world of euphemisms. The real conversations lay under the surface of the polite ones. *He* didn't say much. We never said a word. The silent steps of stairs. Not a creak.

I'd clear my throat to say … Sis, did he, to you, did he? But I couldn't appall her with the sound of it, the meaning of it. And who knows, maybe it's all in my head, these fragments that tail off. I got brave. *Such and such's father interfered with them. Do you think … ?* Interfere, now there's a word. Her mouth went sour. *You're sick!* End of conversation. Say no more. She avoided me for a while but she needed me for something soon enough. It was glossed over. I'm not too sick in the head to feed her cat. Or whatever it was. So where could I go with it? My whole life people acted like the truth, as I knew it, was not the truth at all. A great worker. Lovely couple. Tragic. Sometimes, I just knew. And nothing could persuade me otherwise. If Sis had a different childhood, so be it. I was glad for her. Sometimes I thought she grew up in another house all together. I never said anything to Ben. Besides, he was a man.

Home he came, from London, after all these years. He'd an accent but not much talk. No wife to be heard of. It was good to see his tanned face and lazy smile. I was proud to stride down town alongside him. Over for two weeks, but he stayed the whole summer. It looked like he didn't want to go back. Despite the letters addressed to him in a woman's hand. They tapered off after a while.

My Rebecca is eleven.

There we were, eating our boiled eggs like a proper family, at the breakfast table, skitting each other. There was none of that in this house when I was a girl. A breeze played on the net curtains, the tap dripped and the air was buttery with toast. I was cutting a crossword from the newspaper with my dressmaking scissors. They're too big for the job. Rebecca was in her school uniform; her first day back. A joke of Ben's set her giggling. Paddy Irish man or something stupid like that. I saw then. The way he looked at her. Ben. It was as though he'd reached across the table. Her mood dropped in a breath. She covered her mouth and stared at her plate. He chatted on but I heard none of it. I knew. Wrong was being done. I sat there unable to swallow, a ball of bread sweetened in my mouth. My brain buzzed and flooded. Rebecca left for school. He went outside to have a smoke. I saw him wander down the garden path, heard a train in the distance.

Maybe I'm mad. It's a seductive thought. It means everything is OK. All is good. But I'm not. The truth is a thin milk light. Take your eye off it, and it disappears. I searched and searched. Over the days, hours and minutes of our summer. That picnic by the river. Walks over the field. The bus trip to the seaside. That carnival in the park. Evening times playing cards. There was nothing. I couldn't find anything. Was it too much under my own nose? There was no one I could ask. How could I put such a notion into words? I sat in front of the crusts, shells and cups. Cast my mind back, again and again. A net to the sea. Turned everything I found over like a pebble, weighed it, and held it up to the light. Felt for flaws in the smoothness. Until it came, came home to me. Retrieved.

He was going out. A grey tie hung loose around his neck. *Come here, I'll show you how to fasten this. You'll have to do it for your husband some day.* I was reading the paper. The fire reddened Rebecca's legs as she stood on tiptoe to follow his instructions. He admired himself in the mirror over the mantle piece and went on down to the pub. You have ABCs on the back of your poor knees, I said. The attention flattered her. He was being nice, not many a grown man would take the time. But his voice....

My mind takes its time between the worlds of dreaming and waking. Always did. His voice. I heard it of a morning. *Becca, come help me with my tie.* And me, still thick with sleep, lids resisting the early light. But I'm sure of what I heard, and that I heard it more than once. Ben never wore a tie. Not since that night, when he showed her how to make a proper knot.

Have I brought all this upon us? Tidied the way? I haven't the strength to leave my chair. I see Rebecca as a baby, lying on a picnic blanket, fat and happy in the summer sun. Nobody but me can really remember her like that. I imagine her back there again, imagine her safe and sound, kicking her legs till a sock dangles. But rain breaks. And with the slow heartbeat of a waking beast, a train rumbles near. Someone has moved my child. She's on the greasy sleepers and long grass waves from the track sides. The train becomes louder. I hobble towards her. A stricken actress from a silent movie, my hands fluttering to my face. My high heel lodges in the gravel. I slip from it to rescue my daughter, hold her tight to my chest. The train passes, lifting my hair.

If I don't do something this minute, someone, him probably, will convince me I'm crazy. That my gut is lying. Who'll protect Rebecca if I'm persuaded against myself? I march down the garden path. Dead breath chases my neck. *Stop, May, the Lord takes care of his own.* Like fuck he does, like fuck. My life is braking inside me. Ben leans in the doorway of the shed. Pity surges my throat. I swallow. He doesn't ask me what is wrong. I stare at him, tears washing my mouth. And still, he doesn't ask.

THE AMERICAN GIRL

Kevin Power

Since winning the Hennessy Emerging Fiction Award for 'The American Girl' *in 2008, Kevin Power has published a novel,* Bad Day in Blackrock, *(2008), which inspired Lenny Abrahamson's acclaimed film,* What Richard Did *(2012). He was awarded the Rooney Prize for Irish Literature in 2009. He recently completed a PhD in American Literature at UCD.*

Tim Adams was a Sandford Academy boy, one of the intellectual ones, which meant that the bookshelf in his bedroom contained the following foxed and beer-stained volumes:

Fear and Loathing in Las Vegas by Hunter S. Thompson
The Catcher in the Rye by J. D. Salinger
American Psycho by Bret Easton Ellis
Naked Lunch by William Burroughs
On the Road by Jack Kerouac
Howl by Allen Ginsberg
Notes from Underground by Fyodor Dostoyevsky

Some of the Sandford boys that year thought they were Holden Caulfield and some of them thought they were the Underground Man. The Holden Caulfield ones sat in corners and conveyed by a tilt of the head or an ironic sneer that they found you phony and that your enjoyment of mixed company was not to be trusted. The Underground Man ones were nervy and told embarrassing stories that did not redound to their own credit.

Tim Adams was an Underground Man. 'This book is the story of my life,' he would say, waving a battered paperback.

Notes from Underground was not the story of Tim Adams's life. Tim Adams was the son of two consultant oncologists and he lived in a comfortable six-bedroom house with two cats and a large conservatory in which he sat every Sunday morning with the newspapers and a cappuccino. His identification with the Underground Man – if you want my theory on it – helped him to do what all middle-class children need to do, which is legitimise the fleeting traumas of a privileged adolescence.

I should explain that by the time of my story, Tim was twenty-one years old and enrolled at UCD. He studied Psychology. He had chosen this subject because the first-year booklist included two novels by Fyodor Dostoyevsky, *Notes from Underground* and *The Gambler*, one of which, by the time I introduced Tim to Kelly Cassidy, he still had not read.

The other important thing is that, during the summer of 2005, Tim's father Henry died of a stroke at the age of fifty-two. At the funeral I could barely look at Tim – funerals have their own economy of respect – but I remember him shaking people's hands with rapid vehemence, as though in thanking people for coming he was aiming to transfer the burden of his grief to someone else, someone better able to bear it than he was.

Tim was the sort of person who throws mulled-wine parties at Christmas, which is why I brought a girl named Kelly Cassidy to Tim's parents' house in Donnybrook on the evening of 17 December 2005. The three chief rooms – hall, kitchen, conservatory – were a triptych of brash cordiality. We moved through college conversations: amateur theatre, blowjobs, *American Psycho*. Lemon halves, the white of their pith discoloured by the wine's prevailing burgundy, bobbed in an enormous basin on the stove.

For Tim, these parties had become the occasions of a wilful martyrdom. He competed with himself in his task of self-abasement. Which embarrassing story would he tell to which beautiful girl? Would it be the story of the time his schoolfriends stripped him naked, locked him out of the house, and called the guards? And would he tell this to the girl with the auburn ringlets and the muscular inch of suntanned belly visible above the crenulated waistband of her Abercrombie tracksuit bottoms? Or would it be the time he got so mashed on pills that the lads found him lying underneath his car at 3 a.m., shouting instructions at an elderly Chinese lady he had commandeered to gun the engine while he tinkered with the brakeline? And would he tell this to the blonde in the denim hotpants who kept stirring her drink with her index finger?

We liked Tim rather, in spite of his conversational masochism. Girls liked him too. They viewed him with that strange combination of amusement and erotic charity of which only women are capable. He had stolen girlfriends – potential and actual – from several of us, and this had made us wary, less keen to condescend.

So when I introduced him to Kelly Cassidy I thought I was waving her goodbye. Although I had known her for less than a week, I had already deduced that she was the kind of girl (sexually neutral, intelligent, American) who would fall like a ton of bricks for the arrogant refinement of Tim's self-loathing.

In the event, this isn't quite what happened.

The first time I took Kelly out for drinks she brought along a tote bag from which she produced, as the evening went on, a collection of books by Jacques Derrida, Slavoj Žižek, Friedrich Nietzsche, and Paul de Man. These books were full of underlinings and Post-it notes. Kelly wanted to talk about them. She wanted to know what I thought.

I wasn't used to this kind of thing. Usually I went out with girls who wore too much eyeliner and kept razor blades in their handbags, girls who said things like, 'Nothing means anything. There's just no meaning, you know?' and 'Just look at the size of my ass.' Kelly Cassidy wanted to talk about Theory (you could hear the capital T) and about whether or not she should pursue a doctorate in Dublin or go back to her native Texas and become a theatre critic.

She took me back to her flat that first evening and went into the bathroom to do whatever it is that women do in bathrooms to prepare themselves for sex. I checked out the bookshelf (Sartre, Kierkegaard, D. H. Lawrence) and sat on the bed feeling drunk and disconnected and glum.

The next morning I walked her to work. As we paused on the corner of Grafton Street I invited her to Tim's party, and immediately regretted it. But she, dimpling her chin, accepted, and I flushed in the cold air with the pleasure of her attention.

I was astonished and proud that she had chosen me. Kelly was the kind of girl that each of my friends – all of them educated at expensive private schools – would have coveted, and won, at my expense. This time I seemed to have beaten them to it.

My friends and I loved American girls. We loved their automatic cultural authority. We loved (and scorned) their even-handed sociability (because we were not even-handed, not in the least; we were a club, an enclave, a cabal). We always had a token Yankee on the go. None of them, thus far, had ever been mine. I knew that Kelly was a risk, a bold presumption. This is why I was nervous about the party. I was worried about what my friends would think.

I didn't go to a private school. I evaded by default the neat taxonomies, the roles and rivalrous partnerships that defined and stimulated the social lives of my college friends. Nor did I grow up in a six-bedroom southside semi with a hundred-metre lawn. During my first few weeks at university I would study these houses as I passed them on the bus – these houses with their sculptured gardens and their broad front doors – and wonder what kind of people could possibly live in them, what kind of boy or girl could possibly be produced by all that luxury and space. Eventually I found out, of course. By the time I entered my second year, the people who lived in those enormous houses had become my friends.

They disliked the girls I chose, these new friends of mine. They found them 'shallow' or 'immature' or 'annoying'. They took me aside at parties to ask, 'So, when are you breaking up with what's-her-face?' It came easily to them, this pragmatism about my life. They had this trait in common: that they could treat their own romantic lives like works of art, objects in need of pruning or revision. It disconcerted me that they should see my life in terms like these.

But I liked my friends. I liked their self-assurance and their polished jocularity. I experienced their acceptance of me as an improbable boon, undeserved and longed-for, like grace. In less than a year, I had come to depend on them.

✲

We crossed the kitchen and wound up in the dining room. People sat or stood with their cans of beer or their paper cups of mulled wine.

'Hey,' I heard someone call across the room, 'is Bob Dylan Jewish, or what?'

From one corner a boy surveyed the party with a look of disbelief, shaking his head every few minutes and mouthing the word *phony*.

I introduced Kelly to the drama gang. I introduced her to the debating gang. I introduced her to Tim Adams, who pumped her hand with brisk, compulsive force (as though she were a mourner at his father's funeral) and said, 'Try the mulled wine. I made it, so obviously it's shit. But try it, just try it, it's a sacrifice, I know, I know. But it's a mulled-wine party, you know, it's Christmas, you drink mulled wine, one drinks mulled wine at Christmas, so I thought I'd try to poison as many of my friends as possible, you know what I mean?'

'I'm cool,' Kelly said, blinking.

'Wise move,' Tim Adams said, nodding quickly, 'wise move. I put in too much nutmeg. I'm expecting casualties. I'm expecting vomit in the sink. Most of which will probably be mine, you know?'

Kelly listened with that quality of placid attentiveness that my friends had always taken to be uniquely American. Tim touched her elbow or her shoulder as he spoke.

'Here,' he said, 'sit down. Sit down beside me. We'll go into the living room so I can embarrass myself in private.'

'I'm cool,' Kelly said again. She indicated me. 'I'm happy here.'

So Kelly and I talked in a corner of the kitchen, half-removed from the centre of the party. I sensed a certain puckish resentment from the drama gang, who liked to snare American girls for productions of American plays. Someone had already approached Kelly and asked her how she'd feel about playing Blanche in next semester's production of *Streetcar*, but Kelly said, 'I don't really act? I just like watching plays, you know?'

At around midnight Kelly left to use the bathroom and I found myself alone. Tim Adams took me into the kitchen and ladled some sour remnants of mulled wine into my glass.

'She's, ah, very hot,' he said. 'Very hot, if I may say so.'

'Thanks,' I said.

'Very withdrawn. Very non-judgemental, if you know what I mean. I suppose that's what she's doing with you. Where'd you meet her?'

'Tutorial,' I said.

'And have you, ah, have you done the deed yet, so to speak?'

'Yep,' I said.

'Well share the wealth, you know what I'm saying? Share the wealth, man!'

Tim laughed and went back into the dining room. He had a coiled and stealthy air that suggested he was about to shift his self-deprecation into a higher gear.

I went outside to have a smoke. Tim's mother had forbidden us to light up in the house. I approved of this but missed the way that after other, more licentious parties, the hairs on your forearms would smell like tobacco when you woke up in the morning.

I stood on the terrace and poured my sour mulled wine into a potted plant. I looked at the empty garden. A tongue of grass protruded as if to lap at the night. The sounds of the party – seismic, murmurous – rose and fell.

When I went back inside Kelly was in the living room with Tim Adams. They were sitting on the massive sofa, amid a rampart of tasselled cushions, and Tim was talking softly, shaking his head and ruefully smiling. I had expected this, of course. Tim would make a play; this was a given. I waited at the door to overhear. Which embarrassment would Tim have chosen? Which moment of gruesome comedy would he proffer in exchange for Kelly's sympathy and attention?

'It was just the worst week of my life,' Tim was saying. 'Just unimaginably bad. You have no idea.'

'Mmm,' Kelly said.

'My mother basically hasn't been the same since. You just don't recover, do you, from losing someone like that.'

'Your poor dad,' Kelly said.

'He was only fifty-two,' Tim Adams said. He put his hand on Kelly's and snuffled. 'And there I am at the funeral, and my fly's open, and I have no idea.'

I must have made a noise, because at that moment Kelly looked up and smiled at me.

'Hey,' she said.

'I was thinking we should hit the road,' I said.

'I'm pouring my heart out here, man,' Tim Adams said. He was crying. Plump tears converged in the stubble of his chin. He stood abruptly and waved at me, as if to ward me off. 'Could you give us a minute alone, like? I mean, could you show me some respect?'

'I should really go,' Kelly said, standing. 'I have work in the morning.'

'Great,' Tim said, sharpening his tone. 'Great. Fine. Go with him. At least his father's still alive.'

Kelly said, 'Listen, take it easy, OK? I'm really sorry about your dad.'

'Fine,' Tim Adams said. 'Yeah, fine.'

Kelly put her hand in mine. We closed the huge front door and stepped out onto Morehampton Road. Above us the moon crouched as if pinned or painted on a raked bed of narrow cloud. I thought about Tim Adams as we waited for a taxi in the cold. I thought about the books in his bedroom and I thought about his forceful handshake. I thought about the one thing I had not expected: that my claim on Kelly's love would so outrage him that he would use his father's death to try to steal her from me.

Eventually a taxi showed up and Kelly and I went home to bed.

PROMISE

John O'Donnell

'Promise' was John O'Donnell's first published short story. Since its publication in 2011, he won the Hennessy Award for Emerging Fiction in 2013 for his short story, 'Shelley', and in 2014 Dedalus Press published his third poetry collection, On Water. *His work has been published and broadcast widely and in addition to his Hennessy Fiction Award, his other awards include the Irish National Poetry Prize, the Ireland Funds Prize and the Hennessy Award for Poetry in 1998.*

They tried so hard to be cheerful. They painted bright smiles onto faces that feared the worst. They told themselves if they were positive, he would be positive as well. Then the door of the ground-floor apartment opened and they stepped inside and saw for the first time the masses of cards and letters. They saw the clutter of equipment, all those wires and tubes and leads and screens. And they saw Neil, sitting amidst all this, like a deposed king waiting for the axe to fall.

Neil noticed how they always recoiled when they saw the chair. He'd flinched himself when his mother wheeled it into the hospital to take him home. The fundraising had started while he was still in the rehabilitation wing; one of the Appeal's first purchases had been the chair. With its padded cushions and headrest, and its specially designed ventilator unit at the back, it looked more like a dentist's chair than those worn-down threadbare versions he'd seen patrolling the wards. The leatherette covers shone and the spokes gleamed. But it was still a chair.

Why had he flinched when he'd seen it? He was leaving the hospital; he was going 'home'. It should have been an occasion for relief (if not celebration). Besides, it wasn't as if he'd thought that he would walk away unaided, away from the bed pans and the bowel evacuations, away from the curious gazes of the other patients and the breezy vigour of the nurses. The doctor had been quite clear. When a second opinion had been sought the new consultant had been clearer still. 'Not possible, I'm afraid. Not after this. Spinal cord, C2. There's always stem cell, I suppose, but I wouldn't plan on anything.'

He looked around the apartment. Angelo, the Filipino nursing assistant, had been busy with the tinsel. 'Brighten the place up for Christmas,' his mother had directed. The diminutive Angelo had set ruthlessly about this task. Ropes of gold and silver adorned pictures, door-heads and window frames; how had he managed to reach up so high? A single, glittering, green hawser hung over the length of the forty-inch TV screen the Appeal had also acquired. 'You'll be able to watch all the rugby on the planet,' they'd assured him, and it was true. With Angelo or Petr (his other nursing assistant; Czech, enormous, wordless) operating the remote, day or night there always seemed to be a match on somewhere. Despite what had happened, he'd continued to watch avidly. He'd never blamed the game. His injury was; well, unlucky. It could have happened anyone. They knew that also, the team-mates and supporters who called to see him a little less often these days than before. Wrong place, wrong time; it could have been any one of them.

When the national side won the Championship the captain and most of the team had visited. They'd presented him with a signed jersey and chatted for more than an hour. He'd known a few of the players from before, from squad sessions together; he'd played on an underage team with one of them. They'd crowded into the apartment; hulking, good-humoured, decent men. There was talk of more fundraising for the Appeal, talk even of a charity CD; much laughter as to who was the worst singer. Once or twice as they'd strolled around the apartment they'd paused to look at the hoists and pulleys and supports, the monitors and charts, the jars of pills. Gesturing towards the chair, they'd made light as best they could; jokes about car insurance, and whether Jeremy Clarkson had invited Neil to make an appearance on *Top Gear*. Each time they took the field these men put their bodies on the line in clashes so intense it hurt to watch; they did not take a step back. But here, surrounded by all the contraptions and appliances, the drugs and the devices assembled to try to hold together the pieces from the wreckage of a life, he could sense their unease, the wordless fear, flickering behind their eyes.

How empty the apartment felt when they had gone! This was the part of visits he hated, the winter silence that descended afterwards. In the bleakness of their absence he always felt lonelier after than before. His mother came every day, carrying more cards and letters. He watched her slit the envelopes one after another, reading out each well-meaning message of support. *'Never give up'*. *'Keep fighting'*. *'We're with you all the way'*. But of course, they weren't.

He sighed. Four o'clock. Simon should be here soon. Six foot three, with a voice like a foghorn, he filled the apartment on his own. 'Now then,' he'd blare, as Angelo looked on in awe, 'what have you been up to today?' They'd met at college, at a training session. Neil was all dodge and feint; Simon was bruise and bash. Rapier, bludgeon. The next day Simon had spotted him walking across the courtyard. 'Neil!' he boomed, oblivious to the two terrified Japanese tourists nearby who in response had dropped instantly to their knees. Neil adored him.

They'd played together through their years in university; Simon scrum-half, Neil out-half. In their last year the college had won promotion to Division One; Neil was top points-scorer. It seemed certain they would soon both play for Ireland. Clubs from across the water had already come discreetly calling. Simon, Neil; Neil, Simon: 'The Odd Couple', one rugby correspondent had dubbed them. In team huddles before games there was a comic incongruity about the pair, Simon looming beside Neil, his arm wrapped brutishly around Neil's neck in awkward solidarity.

He could hear Angelo clattering about in the kitchen, the radio tinkling out songs of peace and joy and snow. Was Christmas that close? This time last year, his mother had asked: 'What do you want for Christmas?' He'd struggled to answer; there was nothing he could think of. Twenty-one years old, his post-graduate degree going fine, the provincial management asking if he'd sign up to play, his room in the little redbrick near the canal he shared with teammates Ricky and Wheels. And Anna; sexy, leggy, sassy. What more was there?

He listened. Outside, distant car-noise, the slish of tyres going by in the rain. The music of movement, of momentum. He'd been out several times. To Mass, his mother pushing him up the side-aisle to the front where she prayed patiently for the miracle to happen. The lads had taken him to matches, to pubs. They'd promised to make sure that he did not miss out. Behind the goalposts he'd inhaled the damp air, listening to the roars of supporters, the thud and crunch of bodies colliding on the field. In the corner of a heaving bar after he would at first delight in the chatter and the clink of glasses, the giddy prancing girls, guffaws of laughter among beery hearty men who sat beside him, taking turns. Sometimes later in the evening one or two young ones would totter over to take a look, moist-eyed with sympathy and vodka. 'You're gorgeous,' gasped one of them once, kissing him on the cheek before returning to her friends. He watched her as she left, a pair of skin-tight jeans disappearing into the maw of the crowd, the night, the life he no longer had.

Anna. They'd been together less than a year before the accident; there was no guarantee it would have lasted anyway. She'd hung on gamely for a while; tearful visits to the hospital, and later to the apartment. But the visits became shorter as she became more and more distracted by what he'd long since realised: that this was it. The pressure-sores and the spoon-feeds, the rhythmic, constant wheezing of the ventilator pumping air in through the hole in his trachea: this was all there was, all there ever would be.

He'd seen it one night on television. Switzerland. It wasn't cheap, as one might expect from a country already providing another kind of final resting-place, the bank-vaults like hidden tombs stacked high with hoarded millions. Obviously the Appeal could never – would never – pay. The Appeal was after all dedicated to keeping Neil alive. But Simon had organised it all; forms, the appointments over there with the Director of the Centre and the counsellors, and the plane tickets to Zurich (one return, the other one-way). All to coincide with the first away international match of the season, against Italy. 'Rome,' Simon had explained to Neil's mother. 'My treat. I promised. Call it a Christmas present.' There'd be no need for Angelo or Petr; he knew what to do and would be with Neil all the time. His mother hesitated initially, but later had agreed. What else could she do, with Neil insisting that this trip meant so much? 'So kind,' she'd smiled, blinking back tears. Simon had smiled back weakly; Neil too.

He couldn't have told them. Couldn't. They would have put a stop to it immediately; he knew also they would have assumed responsibility for his intentions, as they had assumed responsibility for everything else in his life. His mother would sob quietly about the sacredness of human life and would redouble her prayers and devotions to the saints. His friends would be stunned, bemused. He imagined them arguing with him: did it take more bravery to die than to live? He could imagine also the hurt, the sadness in the eyes of the Appeal volunteers. He would be begged and hectored and implored to think again. But he *had* thought about this, again and again and again. It wasn't the pain; the drugs worked, mostly. He had every gadget going. He even had enough money, for the moment. What he didn't have was a future.

Simon had refused point-blank at first. 'No way, absolutely no way; you're on your own on this one.' *Exactly*. Neil had wept then, one of the few times since he'd left the hospital, wept as he'd explained that although he'd made the decision on his own, he couldn't do it on his own. Simon had pleaded. 'Ask your mother then. Ask your sister. Not me.' But Neil had persisted. 'You're the only one I know who'll say yes, the only one I trust.' More than anything else in life he wanted this, and only Simon could deliver. His mother, his sister; out of the question. Angelo or Petr; no. Even if either had been tempted by the substantial cash offer he'd considered, they'd be … just wrong.

The facilities offered by the Centre seemed excellent. A room the size of a really good hotel room, with a table and chairs where 'those you wish to accompany you' could sit for a last drink if you wished. And a bed. There was a medical assistant standing by, and a counsellor who was obliged to speak with you in advance on the same day 'to make sure you were proceeding freely with your decision'. Well, 'freely'; what did that mean? But certainly it was his decision, his alone. He'd even promised Simon he'd leave a note, taking all responsibility, apologising for what would seem to some like cowardice. Absolving Simon from all blame. And Simon, exhausted, had relented. They both knew the promise of exoneration meant nothing; that always afterwards there would be fingers pointed at Simon: *You could have stopped him.* Simon would carry this burden from now on, just as he would carry Neil from the chair for the last time, carry him to the pristine-sheeted bed beside a window that gave out onto snow-covered mountains reminding him of Christmas.

There had been ten minutes left to go in the game. They'd been leading by seven points; Neil was certain they'd win. A big forward had come round the back of a scrum, trundling straight at him; he'd tackled him, and they'd gone down. Others arrived on either side to join the heaving mass of limbs scrabbling for the ball. He'd fallen slightly awkwardly, but wedged in at the bottom he'd felt quite safe, waiting for the ruck to end. One of the opposition was raking him, hip, thigh, leg with his boot. The studs dragged across his shorts, his flesh, his socks; it hurt and would hurt more later, but he'd been here before. And then he'd heard a roar of protest from his own side, a deep sonorous voice he knew so well swearing vengeance as it thundered into the ruck. Everything changed then; the new impetus driving the opposition back, driving Neil's body forward, forward, forward – except for his head and neck, which had remained pinned against the dewy grass, the cold earth. He thought he'd heard a click; the vertebrae in his neck cracking under the pressure, unable to hold his spinal cord in place. The referee had whistled immediately, a short panicky blast, which meant things were bad. The last voice he heard before he'd blacked out had been Simon's; nervous, anxious, contrite, promising him it wasn't serious. Promising that the stretcher and the straps and head-brace the emergency personnel were expertly fitting into place were only a precaution. Promising Neil that, no matter what, everything would be fine.

COW TIPPING

Oona Frawley

After 'Cow Tipping' was published in 2009, Oona Frawley concentrated on writing academic books until her novel Flight *became Tramp Press's first publication in April 2014.* Flight *was nominated for an Irish Book Award in the newcomer category. She also contributed a story to the award-winning* Dubliners 100 *(2014) and is currently writing a new novel.*

Julianna went on a road trip with her mom one summer to visit her mom's sister in Iowa, and then all of them drove to Arizona to see her grandfather. She was gone for three weeks, the longest she'd ever been away since they usually only went to the Jersey Shore for a week in July. I got postcards and she was so bored. Nearly the biggest thing that happened was that her mom took a picture of her standing at the spot where four states meet: Arizona, New Mexico, Colorado and Nebraska. She hated it: the driving, the grass, the bugs, and of course it was weird for her meeting her grandfather for the first time the way he didn't know she was black. He was all right about it after the first few minutes, but it sounded like it kinda shook up the retirement community a little bit when this coffee-coloured girl stepped out of the camper van after her pale-as-white-bread mom and aunt.

She met one teenager, her cousin Aaron, in Iowa, who didn't like house or rap and so wasn't as impressed as he should've been about Jule's beatboxing. He was older than her, maybe eighteen, and it tripped him out too having a black cousin, but for him it was like cool. He brought her out one night to the movies with his friends and they also thought she was cool and when he saw that he got her to beatbox for them and she was like oh no oh no and then, being Jule, did it and then they were asking her how to do it and how she learned and she ended up even giving them a dance lesson in the dark after the movie and telling them about L. L. and Bismarky. And it sounds like it helped that she also liked Bon Jovi a little bit ('He's cute, he's all 'ight, I could go there,' she always said), since they all had their hair like that with the whole feather thing going on and the cowboy boots. Only thing was, Jule said, out there their dads wore boots too, so it was hard to tell if it was like a style, or just the way things were.

She asked them about cow tipping because that was what we'd heard they did for fun out there and they laughed and said they did go cow tipping sometimes but they didn't go while Jule was still there. On her last night in Iowa they were supposed to but while she was getting ready to go out her littlest cousin barged in the door of her room and it bumped into Jule's hand while she was using her curling iron. It ended up she burned her eye and drove all the way to Arizona with an eyepatch and the picture at the four corners is Jule wearing some fluorescent orange shorts, a matching tank top, black rubber bangles, her new Creeper shoes, the ones with the splotch of cow-print, actually, and a big old pair of sunglasses, but you can still see the edges of the eyepatch.

She came home and I had never seen her so happy to be back with her dad before: she was like, he ain't that bad y'all. Rather him in New York than a dandy daddy in a cornfield, know what I'm saying?

We got stoned that night since she'd been straight for the whole three weeks – didn't even smoke cigarettes, since her mom didn't want her smoking around her cousins and didn't want her grandfather to know she smoked period. So we got some smoke and she told us about the cornfields and how she was like Mom, how the hell did you LIVE here? No wonder you got your ass on that bus to New York back in the day. No wonder you even put up with That Man.

Jule was the only one of us who talked like that and talked to her mom like that. Then, anyway.

She told us about the movie theatre, a drive-in, and we said no way and didn't believe her. You think I'm lying, she nodded, just wait for the pictures, y'all, that's all I got to say. And it was a drive-in: a big car park in the middle of the fields. So maybe that's where they had sex, really: in their cars.

Rural teenagers, we imagined, had sex in fields. High, thick prairie grasses waved in the night air just like that sea of arms at a stadium rock concert, swaying in unison from side to side until a change in the wind broke the movement and the sway drifted in a different direction: these vast flat fields of middle America that my friends and I could only picture, really, from the *Little House* re-runs we'd seen after school. When there was a story on the news about drought or flooding and stuff there were always these barns sticking up out of the landscape, a lot of times blood red with white edges, or else metal, tinsel silvery in the midst of all of that yellowness of wheat, grass, crops. We didn't know anything about crops, of course. Well, except Easton, whose mother was a botanist and was into flower arranging, which really wasn't the same thing anyway. So it was hard for us to picture teenagers living There generally, in that expanse of space that was so empty, marked like a map of itself with ribbons of road going on for thousands of miles. And then we wondered where in that Space they could have sex.

I don't know, Jule said, so stoned now she was beyond laughter, just staring down at the river and the red and orange lights from Queens stretching tentatively towards Manhattan. I don't think they do have sex, she said blankly. Aaron says things like, 'You're joshing me, Julianna, you're only joshing.' Can you imagine someone like that having sex?

The next day Jule came up to my apartment and then we went to sit in the staircase so we could smoke cigarettes. I'm worried, though, she said to start the conversation (Jule always started conversations with me like that, maybe because we lived only a few floors apart and were always talking).

My mom gone and invited Aaron and that mad little girl to come visit and I swear to god, they gonna come and you watch, I'm gonna have to take Aaron out with me: you watch, my mom's gonna make my ass take that blond-you-joshing-me-boy out.

I laughed. So what? So he comes out. He's not coming to live with you.

Well, she said, it's all right with you guys, but I'm not taking him like out out. Not to the Tunnel or anything, not nowhere like that. He can come hang on the stoops, but no no no no nooo I am not having him at some club with me trying to do my thang and he all in my space saying 'erm, excuse me, Julianna, don't you think that boy is getting a little too close to you?'

C'mon, I said, you met my weird cousin Olivia last year. She managed. Not her scene, but she managed.

Jule erupted in laughter. She managed alright, only cus she got so motherfucking drunk she went home to bed. I still don't know how your moms didn't notice.

I guess she didn't know Olivia well enough to know.

True, Jule said. You walked in like that she woulda gone upside your head. Don't you know, I said.

The next week Jule got word: they were coming. Her aunt Leona, her cousin Aaron, and the little girl who'd given Jule the eyepatch, Mimi. (Imagine that, Jule had said when her mother told her she had a cousin named Mimi: who the fuck names their child Mimi in this day and age?) She came upstairs as soon as her mom got off the phone with the news.

Oh man, she moaned. It's like they all gone family mad or something: we go out there, then we all go to my grandfather, now they all gotta come here. Next thing you know my mother gonna want to go back there and I'll spend the rest of my days the only homegirl in Iowa.

When're they coming? I made Jule tea. In her house they only had Pepsi and milk and Tropicana, so she always felt soothed if I made her tea; she thought it was quaint or something and because my mother was Irish, which it was. No other families had tea like we did.

Two weeks, she stirred sugar gloomily.

And in two weeks, there they were. And whatever Jule was she wasn't a liar: Aaron's language was straight out of a movie. He was like 'wow!' at everything, at the buildings, the elevator (of which Mimi was terrified), the view of the Empire State Building from Jen's living room. Jen brought him straight up to me since she didn't know what else to do with him and he said wow again when he saw the view from my living room, even though it was exactly the same only three floors higher. He thought it was crazy that we had a pool in the building and was nervous swimming on his back because he could see all the buildings around it through the glass ceiling. He had corn yellow hair ('See? I told y'all,' Jule whispered to me, 'all that corn is seriously *in* him.') that was down to his shoulders, cowboy boots and jeans and button-down flannel shirts that were way too hot for New York in August. He was polite and nice, actually, but man he just couldn't contain his awe of the place.

Jule was smoking in front of him now – she had told her mom that there was no way she'd agree to quitting for a week while she had to deal with bringing Aaron around with her – and he occasionally tried to tell her how bad it was for her.

Yes, Aaron, thank you, Jule said, smoke streaming through her nostrils as she examined her fake nails.

I wouldn't want to see you get sick, Julianna, that's all, Aaron said, almost wounded, but not quite; he didn't seem to get a lot of stuff.

She brought him to the Village and dragged me with her, brought him out on the stoops, where he said little and stared when someone eventually lit a joint and a few forties were opened. But she kept insisting to her mom that he wasn't coming to the Tunnel. No way.

But his last evening rolled around and Jule started to cave; she was too nice. All 'ight, Aaron, she said. We going dancing: you wanna come? A nightclub, you know.

We got there and found friends and Jule introduced him. Aaron from Iowa, she announced, meet everyone. Here you go, y'all, she said, introduce yourselves.

Ooohh, Jule, you been keeping him a secret all fo' yourself, Natasha said, heading over to Aaron, who was staring at the way his white T-shirt was glowing.

I should've thought of you, Tash, Jule said: you and your all-American boy thang, I should've thought of you.

And we headed to the dance floor.

Only an hour or so later did we start looking for him. Won't be hard, Jule said, look for the cornfield. But we couldn't find him.

Anyone seen Natasha? I started asking everyone we knew.

Yeah, someone finally said, I saw her go upstairs – upstairs – with some guy.

Upstairs, Jule repeated.

Upstairs, yo.

She didn't, I said.

Oh but I think she did, Jule said.

Upstairs was actually outside, up the stairs, yes, and then out the emergency exit door that was often propped open on hot nights, onto a fire escape. We went up slowly, not talking, following the route; we'd both been down it before.

Man oh man, Jule murmured under her breath.

From the dark end of the hallway we could see the city light coming in through the door, wedged open. We went a little ways down and then could start to hear the cars and the voices drifting up from the street, feel the air coming in; our clothes were clinging to us from dancing and it was so hot inside that the midnight August air felt good. And then we could kind of hear, and then kind of see, and there was Aaron's white ass glowing like his shirt in the semi-dark.

Jule stopped dead and turned to me. I so didn't need to see that, she said loudly. I so didn't need to see someone's white Iowa ass bobbing up and down.

I could see that the ass had stopped bobbing and saw Tash's eyes craning to see in the door.

Hurry up, I said to her, and then steered Jule back down the hall. C'mon, let's have a drink.

Jule paused for a minute. Well, she said loudly again, he's only been joshing me: I guess he's doing some cow tipping.

We burst out laughing.

2010

MACAW

Eileen Casey

Eileen Casey received the Hennessey Award for Emerging Fiction in 2010 for 'Macaw', having been previously shortlisted two times for the Hennessy Awards: for poetry in 2004 and first fiction in 2005. Her debut collection of poems, Drinking the Colour Blue, *was published by New Island in 2008 and her other books include a debut collection of stories,* Snow Shoes *(2012). She has been awarded a Patrick Kavanagh Fellowship and an Arts Council bursary. Her story 'Beneath Green Hills' appears in* All Over Ireland: New Irish Short Stories, *edited by Deirdre Madden and published by Faber & Faber in 2015.*

Louise struggles to stay in the dreaming space but her daughter's persistent voice tugs her back from its weightless cocoon. She surfaces from underneath the duvet just as Lori herself appears around the bedroom door.

'Mam, it's Saturday and you promised …' Lori looks even younger than her sixteen years. Her hair is swept in an up style, loose silky tendrils brushing her shoulders. Her fluffy dressing gown is pulled tight, revealing the curves of her slender body.

'Dad's been up ages and gone for bread, there's mould on what's left in the breadbin, yeuch!' A slight frown steals some of her prettiness.

'Sorry, I thought we had plenty,' Louise says through a half yawn. Her head throbs a little. She's sorry now she'd had that third glass of wine and hates the lingering tang it leaves in her mouth.

'Dad will get lovely fresh rolls, he'll be back soon, I'll shower and get dressed and be down in a minute, OK?'

'OK. But don't forget your promise, it's Jo-Anne's sleepover next ...'

'Friday ... I know, as if I needed reminding, it's all you've been able to talk about ... '

'... And I don't want to look like a skaaanger ...' Lori interrupts, drawing out the word as if holding her breath, enjoying the look on her mother's face.

'What did I tell you about words like that?'

'You're just old fashioned, Mam, everyone says it ... and you had your day on Wednesday, remember?'

'Just give me a few minutes, I need to shower first. I'll come down soon.' Lori nods then sticks her earphones in, already mouthing the words of a song and bouncing her body out of the room. Louise flops her arm across to Dave's side of the bed, the sheet cold under her skin. A few hours earlier he'd reached for her, caressing the small of her back, but when his hand moved along the length of her thigh she bucked her body against him. He'd turned away abruptly, falling into sleep again as she had, out-sleeping him by at least an hour she guessed from the quality of the light and the raucous sound of the neighbourhood 'barbers'. 'Saturday mowers, Lou, worse than Sunday drivers,' Dave often says.

Hot water slicing over her back is a sensation Louise normally savours for as long as possible but her arms swish so fast with sponge and suds that her body is a blur, as if legs, belly and breasts belong to someone else. She sluices off the razor blade left on the soap tray. Lori began shaving her legs a few months before, despite the warnings it would grow back twice as thick and not necessarily blonde either. Unwanted hair. Surely the bane of every woman's life? Like a secret, no knowing when it would find you out, Louise thinks, rubbing steam from the mirror and plucking with her tweezers a stray hair from underneath her eyebrow line. Dave's voice drifts up to her. She imagines him filling the kettle, plugging it in, waltzing the cups to the table, adding side plates, cutting up the rolls, rubbing his hands briskly. She splashes a rush of cold water onto her face and rubs a towel over it vigorously until it stings.

'So … what time are my girls off to town?' he asks, lifting the teapot and pouring the dark liquid into Louise's cup.

'I can give you a lift to the Luas, no problem.' Louise smiles at him, relieved he bears no outward grudge at least over her earlier rejection of him.

'I think we'll go local, I was in town the other day, I don't think I could face it again …'

'And you came home empty handed, not even a pair of tights,' Lori reminds her, shooting her mother a look of total bewilderment.

'I was meeting a friend,' Louise says, busying herself with sugaring her tea. 'Not parading around shops.'

'Maybe you'll find something you like today,' Dave says, stirring one full spoon into his own brew. His eyes meet hers across the breakfast table and for a fleeting moment his mouth tightens. But the moment passes and he recovers his good humour.

'Here, Lou, have some more roll, you'll need all your strength.' He winks at Lori and playfully punches her shoulder. They eat in silence, each absorbed in their own thoughts, listening with half an ear to the news and weather forecast. There's a faint crackle but none of them move to adjust the tuning knob. Lori's expression clearly shows she's already in shopping paradise, her earphones draped around her neck ready to be pushed into her ears the minute her breakfast's eaten. Despite her warm fleecy tracksuit Louise shivers. No matter what the position of the sun or the time of the year, there always seems to be a chill in the house, like cool to the touch cotton sheets. The sun just never reaches farther than half-way up the garden. Sometimes, there's only the tiniest patch of it. Lori used to say, 'I'll pull down the sun for you, Mam. I'll get a big lasso and pull it down towards the kitchen window until the whole place is toasting.' Was it only a year go since Lori said that? 'Been watching *Bruce Almighty* again have we?' Louise would say, tousling her daughter's hair. Lori was growing up for sure, moving into teenage bras, lipstick, 'growing her feathers' as her mother used to say and testing out how much cheek she could get away with.

Louise looks at the pile of washing waiting in the laundry basket to be loaded into the machine and wonders if there's any powder left in the box. It's got a mermaid on the front, a sea woman with long hair and a big fishy tail, swishing about in a cloud of bubbles as if washdays were for blowing bubbles while the machine rocked from side to side, vibrating down through the floorboards. Nine out of ten women prefer this brand, so the jingle goes. Nine out of ten women prefer clear, perfectly formed bubbles that were just the right weight, the right buoyancy, resilient yet graceful.

'I'll run this lot through while you're gone,' Dave says, noticing the direction of her gaze. 'No sweat.' He wipes his mouth with a paper napkin and slides out of the chair, turning off the radio with a grimace of disgust.

'Nothing only bad news as if there's not enough,' he says, already gathering up the delph, stacking it neatly on the sink. He's all movement lately, hardly able to sit still long enough to eat. There's been talk of lay-offs in work, but as usual he's only told her the bare minimum.

Half an hour later Louise is sitting on a shoe shop bench watching Lori try on sneaker after sneaker. Lori tries on high heels too, 'just for the laugh', walking up and down as if auditioning for *America's Next Top Model.* Lori could be on the red carpet she seems so poised, so unselfconscious. Like those gorgeous girls Louise saw on the Golden Globes. Beautiful, with low-cut evening gowns. It still strikes her as funny in an odd sort of way. The Golden Globes on the television, in a waiting room filled with women just like herself, most of them around the same age, others young as Lori almost. Women with husbands or partners at their side, holding their hands or absently rubbing the inside of their wrists. Others like her, on their own. The silence, apart from the television droning, is stifling in the high-ceilinged room. Louise is glad Dave's not there. She knows he's definitely not one of the nine out of ten husbands who prefer to be there … even if he knew she was there in the first place. He wouldn't be happy sitting so still for so long. He'd fidget, need to go out for air or just to walk up and down the busy street watching taxis take off from or land at the kerb, as if they were aeroplanes at a busy terminal. He'd be shaking out cigarette after cigarette, blowing smoke all over passer-bys, the same way he did the night Lori was born. Louise was glad to be on her own in the grey-carpeted, colour-muted room, watching the Golden Globes, not knowing whether to laugh or cry.

'I really like these, Mam … Mam … you haven't been listening to a word!' Lori nudges her arm, bringing Louise back into a shop full of shining shoes, unpaired, their partners in tissue-packed boxes.

'We agreed on forty euros max,' she says, unable to keep tension out of her voice. 'These are nearly twice that.'

'They'll last twice as long, Mam, you know they will,' Lori replies in a wheedling tone.

'You get what you pay for,' the assistant chips in, seizing the moment with years of professional practice behind her.

'You get what you pay for,' Louise repeats as she punches in the number of her credit card with more force than she intended.

Two changing rooms later and each time she sees her daughter in another outfit Louise is reminded of an exotic bird, so painfully beautiful that to look at its startling shades hurts her eyes. The boutique fills up with other young women, glossy hair, pouting lips, their scent mingling in a heady cocktail. All of them wanting something new to wear, something that will show off their ripening curves, float them over their ordinary lives, at least for the weekend. Colours that brighten the dimmest nightclub and restaurant or swirling onto bedroom floors in the heat of a moment. Louise blushes, an old habit from years back that still plagues her. She lowers her head and hopes Lori hasn't noticed but already her daughter is gone behind the changing room curtain, shucking out of yet another outfit Louise decides is 'too old' for her. In the end, a compromise is reached.

'Thanks, Mam, you're the best,' Lori says when they reach home. Dave has the fire started, which is a welcoming sight.

'Grateful enough to pull down the sun for me?' Louise asks. Her throat feels tight as if the old words are suddenly too big. Lori looks abashed but only for a moment. She playfully hugs her mother and says 'definitely!' before scampering upstairs with her treasures. Louise sinks into an armchair and eases her feet out of her shoes. She notices the shiny secateurs on the coffee table, its heavy silver head shaped like the beak of a parrot.

'It's time that overgrown triffid in the driveway got the chop, Lou. It's practically out of control … and scratching the side of the car,' Dave says with a grimace. The car is his pride and joy, washed and polished religiously, rolled out like a limousine from their narrow driveway for taking Lori to sleepovers.

'Sit by the fire and warm yourself,' he says, 'I'll be done before you know it. See if there's anything on the box for later.' She looks up at him and he seems to be a great distance above her, his head like a small, dark disc. Perhaps she could tell him now? But before she can say anything he takes up the secateurs, its size and shape making an awkward fit in his hand.

She closes her eyes, sees again the room with the chairs lined up against the wall, the acrid smell of geraniums drifting from the window sill, a smell reminding her of grief and anger. Her mother always had geraniums, her green fingers coaxing them from the smallest slips, dead-heading faded blooms to encourage healthy plants. Their scent permeated the small council house she'd grown up in. Her mother died when Louise was in her teens, her body shrivelled, her illness detected too late to save her. Her father had shrivelled up too, and threw out all the geraniums saying he couldn't bear the sight of them.

She hears Lori moving around overhead, dancing her body into the small spaces between the furniture. Another sound comes, faint at first but as Dave moves nearer to the house, she hears the distinct clip of the steel cutting through the tender branches of her cotoneaster. She feels a sharp sensation in her right breast and her hand closes protectively around it. Its familiar softness surprises her briefly. What had she expected? Dave would be thorough, pruning back to the boundary wall, removing all unwanted leaf and bud, practicality over sentiment winning the day.

She wonders what Clark Kent, at least that's what he looks like to her, is doing. Probably playing with his children, or just relaxing with his wife over a pre-dinner drink. Why shouldn't he? After all it was the weekend, he was only human, certainly no superman, no matter how much he resembled Clark Kent with his thick black hair and glasses. Why should he be sitting in his oak wood office on a Saturday afternoon, drawing diagrams for a virtual stranger? First a small circle then a biggish one as if an eclipse were taking place, one circle threatening to obliterate the other. He spoke in such measured tones they might be discussing the weather instead of the results of the call back screening, patterns of family history, statistics, choices of treatment, possible outcomes.

All the while he is speaking to her, Louise's eyes stray to the photos of his wife and children on the bookshelf behind his desk. Their faces lit up, the children wearing summer clothes: sailor-type shirts and little pleated skirts. Perhaps the photo has been taken in their own backyard, sun flooding the whole way up, not just over a patch, barely big enough for a young girl like Lori to stand in, her head titled back, temporarily out of reach from the shadows working their way relentlessly around her. Clarke's wife wears a straw hat that freckles her face. Louise will wear hats, she decides, she couldn't bear the thought of someone else's hair. Or she will buy a bright turban the same shade as a scarlet macaw, its vivid colour startling the paleness of her skin. And they have good insurance, treatments were more advanced now. Her heart beats wildly at the thought of telling Dave. If not today, then definitely tomorrow she decides. When he eventually comes in from the garden, the secateurs are gripped in his hand, stray wisps of green trailing from the blade.

'That should hold it. For another while at least,' he says, 'You know how Lori complains when it snags at her clothes.' Louise notices the tired look on his face, the awkward lean of his body against the doorframe. But she must tell him and now is as good a time as any. The ticking in her chest is like a time-bomb, so loud she thinks it will burst. Words form in her mouth, fragile, distorted, not the ones nine out of ten women prefer. Words that wobble and awkwardly teeter around the edges before breaking apart.

CAPRICORN

Kevin Doyle

Since Kevin Doyle's story was published on the New Irish Writing page, a mini-collection of short stories about the Heavy Gang era in Irish politics, Do You Like Oranges?, *has appeared. He was runner-up in the Sean Ó Faoláin Prize (2013) and is currently working on a novel set in Cork. His website is www.kevindoyle.ie.*

Peader Hallisey looked along the shimmering streak of black bitumen and pulled on to the Northern Highway. The road was quiet and he headed south, the sun behind him at last. After a mile or so he pulled over, onto the hard shoulder and coasted slowly. Scanning the desert he finally saw the rock, peering over a clump of bottlebrush; in the intense sunlight it almost glowed.

Applying the brakes, the truck skidded to a halt on the dusty verge. He left the engine to idle and got out into the bright sunshine; it was like stepping into an oven. Looking around he saw dots of parched spinifex grass spreading across the plain of red sand. Further away there was a cluster of ant hills and beyond these, near the dry river bed, a deep gash in the hillside – a place the aborigines called the Innarara.

Eighteen years earlier Hallisey had been shown this place by an elder of the Banjima tribe, a man named Thomas Bass. He had trekked with Bass for almost a month through the wilderness of the Pilbara, avoiding the big mining towns of Newman and Marble Bar. Bass had shown him the aborigine landscape and explained that it was custom to ask permission of the ancestors whenever one crossed onto their lands – lands that were not marked on any map of western Australia but that were there nonetheless.

Hallisey stepped forward now and shouted clearly, 'I ask the permission of the ancestors to pass through these lands of the Banjima people.'

His statement was met by a pervading silence. Even so Hallisey remained a moment listening, until a long road-train passed him on the opposite side of the highway, its after-draft pummelling him and his vehicle.

Climbing back into the truck's cabin, he closed the door and cooled in the air-conditioning. A short while later he was back out on the road; he had about thirty miles to go.

A week earlier Hallisey had been out delivering supplies for the Shire in the lands around Jigalong, not far from the Rabbit-Proof Fence. He had come home from the long drive to find the light blinking on his answering machine – a rare occurrence. He pressed the button to listen. It was a voice from a long time ago. The Cork accent was strong and gravelly; the tone slightly jubilant. It was Tony Barrington. He began, *I was in Dublin yesterday ...* The message explained about a report that had just come out in Ireland about the industrial schools and what had gone on in them. Hallisey listened to the entirety of the long message. He didn't really know what to make of its suddenness. Here, so far away, he hardly knew anything any more about what was happening in the world, let alone back in Ireland.

He showered, listened to the message again and then went out onto his veranda to watch the sun set – something he did most evenings. Later, before going to bed, he listened to the message again. This time he took down the details.

✲

He saw the Capricorn Roadhouse ahead, on a wide clearing. The road stop was like an oasis – a place to get petrol, to stretch the legs and to take a shower. It was the nearest settlement of any size to Hallisey, who lived by choice in the remote outback. The current manager, a Torres Strait islander by the name of Lance Cooper, was a good friend of his. Earlier he had phoned Cooper to tell him that he was on his way in.

Pulling off the highway, Hallisey drove slowly up the unsealed track that led to the forecourt, stopping as near as he could to the ugly white awning that afforded generous shade. Switching off the engine, he collected his cigarettes and got out. Again he felt the blast of dry heat.

Lighting up, he took a long deep draw. Civilisation? Certainly it was the largest human conurbation for a hundred miles in any direction. And it was busy today. There was a large camper van pulled in at the pumps. Lines of road-trains were parked in parallel in the truckers' compound. Near him a Landrover was being kitted out for serious off-road driving. Jerrycans marked 'Drinking Water' were neatly lashed to the sides and on the roof Hallisey spied one of the new GPS dishes that he had heard the Shire workers talking about. He saluted the driver casually and she smiled at him.

Finishing his cigarette, he stamped on the butt and entered the roadhouse. 'Aaah,' he said to the immediate effect of the air-conditioning. It felt glorious – one of the great inventions, he believed. He felt like raising his arms up high to let the air in, but didn't.

Cooper had new posters up about the Freemantle Dockers – the A. F. L. footie team from down Perth way that Cooper adored. They were having another bad season – Hallisey would point that out to him.

He was hailed from behind the counter. 'OK mate,' said Hallisey, returning the wave. He indicated that he was fine to hang about for a while.

At the self-service coffee machine he made himself a cup of black coffee using three espresso shots. Taking a seat by the window, he watched the goings on out in the forecourt. It was tough driving territory and anyone who was here at the Capricorn was happy to take their time before hitting the long road once more.

He drank his coffee and examined a slip of paper that he had taken from his breast pocket. There was an address on the paper – not that it looked like an address. 'Address' was the term Barrington had used in his phone message. Hallisey had faithfully recorded each letter and number of this 'address', which Barrington had said he should take to an internet cafe. Cooper was Hallisey's internet cafe.

'That's three cups of coffee you had there,' said his friend when he finally came over. 'Don't think that I didn't see what you did. You'll have to pay for all three.'

'Put it on my tab,' said Hallisey.

'Your tab is closed.'

They both smiled and Cooper put his hand out to clasp Hallisey's in welcome. 'So what brings you to town, Irishman?'

Hallisey handed him the slip of paper. 'Does that make any sense to you? Seems I can listen to it.'

'So the internet has caught up with you at last, old man. Where did you get this from?'

'A friend from way back. Phoned me up with it. Said I could listen to it?'

Cooper scrutinised the slip. 'It's an audio file, OK. Podcasts they're called. Something from the radio most likely.' He paused. 'Though occasionally it can be phone sex stuff too.'

'That's most likely it,' grinned Hallisey.

'I figured.'

✲

Cooper set up Hallisey on the computer in the back office. He helped him type in the internet address but they made an error and nothing happened. They checked it and made one correction. On the second attempt it loaded.

'Play, pause, stop,' said Cooper, showing Hallisey with the mouse which icon was which. 'Just like in the old tape decks,' he added with a guffaw and thumped the Irishman's shoulder.

Hallisey was left alone. He waited. There was intro music and an announcement. The programme was called *Liveline* and the presenter was talking to people on a march in Dublin. It was called the March of Solidarity and a woman explained that she had come all the way from the States to be there, in Dublin, at the march. Hallisey then heard a man being interviewed. He told his story in a plain, unemotional voice. He was abused at an industrial school he was sent to while preparing for his first Holy Communion.

Hallisey paused the recording. The noise and chatter from the counter outside receded and he felt his heart thump. After waiting a moment he clicked the play button again. The next person interviewed, another man, was much more edgy and angry. As he spoke, there was shouting and cheering in the background from the march. There were more interviews and then Hallisey recognised his friend. Barrington began strongly but his voice grew quieter as he went on. He told about their school in Cork – Greenmount Industrial School. He said it out: what had happened to him there, the exact details. Hallisey hardly heard anything from that point on.

In forty-three years Hallisey had been back to Ireland only once – in 1991. That time he had stayed with his sister – she was now dead. He went by the old place where he had lived. Then he made one effort to walk out to Greenmount School but didn't make it. Instead he caught the bus and went up to Galway. He wanted to see the beautiful Ireland that they all talked about in Australia. He didn't go back to Cork.

After he returned to Australia, something had changed for Hallisey. The outback was different. Just as Ireland was more than what it appeared as on the surface, so also was Australia.

Soon after Hallisey moved out of Perth permanently and got work up north in the Pilbara, at one of the mines. But it wasn't what he wanted to do. He took a variety of jobs after that – as a shearer, as a handyman and later as a farm mechanic. It was during those years, traipsing back and forth across the Pilbara, that he learned about the true history of the area and the different people who lived there – the Banjima, Yindjibarndi, Birrimaya, Ngaluma, Jaburara.

He gravitated deeper into outback; the remoteness and solitude drew him.

Cooper came in with a coffee. He saw the Irishman staring into space. There were tear streaks on his dusty brown face and the computer was silent. He put his hand on Hallisey's shoulder and left it there. Hallisey put his hand up onto his friend's to acknowledge it.

'I guess it's not phone sex then.'

'No.'

A while later Hallisey finished with the podcast. He got up, went out to the cafe and took his seat again by the window.

Cooper came over eventually. 'It's on the house, what do you want?'

'A can of your coldest Solo.'

Cooper returned with the lemonade drink and a straw. He explained, 'I got you the straw because you're such a baby.'

Hallisey didn't respond. He looked down, pulled the tab and took a long slug from the can.

'Why don't you hang about?' said Cooper. 'When Jenny comes on later we can take off and have a beer. Wouldn't that be an idea?'

'I might just do that,' said Hallisey.

He went outside, this time to the back of the roadhouse to where the well-known tourist attraction was. A metal rail like a single train track had been embedded long-ways in the red earth. The rail was polished from people walking on it and it glinted in the sunshine. A sign nearby said *This Is The Tropic Of Capricorn.*

Hallisey went and leaned against the sign. He was glad now of the hot sun. Staring out over the flat red outback, he thought about Barrington. He recalled an event a long time ago. He was sitting with his friend on the bank of the Lee, just under the Shaky Bridge. It was one of those times when they had run away from Greenmount. They were looking at the slow-moving, silent flow of water. Suddenly Barrington began rocking back and forth the way a child might. His head was buried in his knees, which he was clasping tightly into himself and he was crying. He wouldn't say what was wrong.

Hallisey had never known exactly what had happened to his friend until now. He had guessed of course, had guessed it was like what had happened to him. But it was never spoken of between them. Instead there had always been just this bond, a bond that allowed a postcard and an odd letter to float between them across the continents over the decades.

The odd thing was, Hallisey thought now, he envied Barrington. In some way, he felt, his friend had freed himself. By saying it out on the radio, in detail, about what had happened to him, wasn't that what he had done? And wasn't it something? Hallisey had never told anyone.

2011

A VIGIL

Andrew Fox

Since his story was published in New Irish Writing under the original title of 'By the Canal', Andrew Fox has published both fiction and journalism in The Dublin Review, The Stinging Fly, The Massachusetts Review *and* The Daily Beast. Over Our Heads, *his debut collection of short stories, which includes 'A Vigil', is published this year by Penguin Ireland.*

Whenever things got too much for me, during those bad years when we lived on Harrington Street, I used to leave the flat and go out walking for as long as it took to get my head together. Usually a quick stomp around the block would do the trick, but sometimes I would be gone for hours, marching in aimless fury or boarding buses with a vague desire to spread my anger thin over distance.

No matter where my rambling took me, though, I'd always finish up in the same place. Before going home I'd buy a pack of cigarettes and sit on a bench by the Grand Canal to smoke a few, end to end. I had a favourite spot: just beyond Baggot Street Bridge, where the towpath sinks below the level of the road and is separated from the pavement by a tall black fence. There I could expect to find the silent company of a drunk embracing a bottle of strong cider, or on weekends that of an unimaginative father watching a son or daughter pelting the swans with bits of bread. I liked it down there. It was a place where you could be by yourself without having to suffer the horror of being alone.

Laura, my wife, was an actor, and she was beautiful. If you had seen us together on the street you would have wondered what she saw in me. The answer was that we shared a secret – call it faith or fantasy. What had bonded us in college was a resolution to deny the signs that neither of us was meant for greatness, and it was this commitment that had tightened us together throughout the ruin of our twenties. What did we fight about? The usual, I suppose. Sex, money, selfishness. *Why* we fought is a far more interesting subject, and a problem that I have never quite been able to solve. It certainly didn't help that we were both only ever partially employed, but I think it went deeper than that. I think it had something to do with needing someone to hate every now and then. It also might have had something to do with needing someone to forgive you. Let's just say that in our own ways we were a source of comfort for each other, through our failures and through our shared loss of youth, and that of lesser things are lasting marriages made.

During the week I turned thirty, I studied the Facebook accounts of old friends who had become actuaries or engineers. That weekend Laura arranged for us to spend a few days in her uncle's caravan in Wexford. We drank spiced rum, played songs on my guitar and ate ice cream topped with hundreds and thousands by the beach. We had a decent time. But on the train home on Sunday afternoon we both were dangerously hung-over. We got to sniping and, as soon as we had climbed the stairs to the flat, we fell into a fight. Laura had left her phone behind in the caravan and, as was her wont whenever faced with a problem that lacked an easy solution, she started stomping around the place, slamming doors and working herself into a tantrum.

'But you don't under*stand*,' she said in response to my attempts at soothing her. 'I'm expecting a *call* this week. I'm expecting my *agent*. I'm expecting *work*. Remember work?'

'Sure I remember work,' I said. 'It's the place I go to every day. And where I'll be tomorrow while you're crying over your fucking phone.'

For these were our established starting positions, the pattern we had well rehearsed. Whichever one of us had a job at any given moment would – as well as paying off the credit cards and buying too much shopping from the good supermarket – assume it as his or her right to lord it over the other. Every now and then, I was a productive member of society while she was a spoiled little girl with silver-screen delusions. And occasionally, she was a pillar of financial stability while I was a fantasist who had never quite got over the time his band had opened for – whoever.

Laura moved to the window and began to smoke violently, her chin thrust forward in her customary challenge to the world. She was wearing a pair of my jeans and her skin still smelled of the beach. Stray strands of her hair seemed to glow in the weakening sunlight.

'I'd hardly call what you're doing *work*,' she said. 'Little office boy. That's fucking drudgery.'

I closed my eyes and breathed slowly through my nose. Something in my jaw was clicking back and forth. I struggled for eloquence. I knew where we would be in a few minutes' time but I forged ahead regardless.

'Sweetheart,' I said as my hand sought warmth at the small of her back. 'Look, it's fine. We'll figure it out. Why don't you just call *him*?'

'Oh, right. Yeah, sure. Perfect.' I could tell that Laura was close to tears. 'You really haven't a fucking clue about the world, have you? You really don't know anything about how things work.'

The traffic noise from the street outside had risen to a horrible pitch. It came like a flood through the open window, pulling with it its grime and its threat and forcing me to see my home for what it was. I looked around at the cheap sticks of inexpertly repaired furniture, the battered TV, the maniac watercolours that Laura and I had made together in a shared fit of painterly enthusiasm as – *wham!* – a bus tore past and filled the room with its roar.

In a blind rage I hit the street and walked without direction. The faces of the people walking towards me – strangers on their way to their evening's destinations, where they would be happy, or not – seemed to possess knowledge of how I was living my life. I retreated to a pizza place on Merrion Row and was reassured for a while by the easy comfort of cheese and grease and dough. I ordered beer and moved on to wine and finished with Amaretto.

When the waitress came over with my bill she smiled in a way that I thought spoke of pity born from a kindred sadness. She had eyes that looked as though they might never be too far away from crying. I noticed that she was wearing a coat.

'You're finished with your shift,' I said.

Her eyes darted to the door.

'Will you have a drink with me, then? It's my birthday. One drink? I even know a place.'

I could see the rest of the night laid out before us. We would go to the canal together with a bottle and talk until dawn, confess our sins and be reborn in one another's mercy. But of course the waitress wouldn't come with me. What she did was call the manager – a fat, oily little creature with a thick bunch of keys hanging from his belt and a name tag that read 'Eugene' pinned over one of his breasts – who escorted me from the premises and suggested that it might be best if I never returned.

So I bought a bottle of supermarket Cabernet and went alone to the canal. There was no one else on the towpath. It was getting dark but the sky held no hope of stars. I found my usual bench and sat down and opened the bottle. The wine was of the kind that coats your tongue and makes you spit blue for hours. I watched the swans, counting and recounting them, and felt as though I had arrived at a moment of great decision. The feeling had an intensity the like of which I had known only once before. That had been many years earlier, but it was a moment to which my mind often returned while sitting by the canal. Laura and I were still spending our Sunday afternoons in bed back then. I had money, and had just returned from the good supermarket with lunch things I knew she'd like. I found her asleep, the sheets pulled back to reveal her narrow shoulder blades and her head resting on an arm, her face turned towards me. I knew for certain that she was my life and decided right then that I would commit myself to the service of her happiness. Now, as I drank, I tried to picture the way Laura's face had looked that day that made me love her. I focused my mind on trying to pull that image forward from my lost years. But it wouldn't come.

The swans moved off together downstream but one stayed where he was. I watched him closely. An enormous cob, his neck was as long as my arm and above his beak there was a fat black bulge that might have been the source of his power. Soon I began to think that he must be trapped or snagged on something. I walked to the edge of the bank and peered down into the dark water, looking for a snarl of rope or wire or a spear of steel broken from a shopping trolley. There was nothing there, and then there was something. Floating into focus, I began to make out another swollen curl of breast and feather on the bed of the shallow canal. I could see an orange foot, a silt-brown tail. I studied the way the water rocked her neck.

The cob circled slowly, his head tucked tightly to his breast. I decided to make an observance. I sat back down and finished my wine and kept him company until dawn. All night he kept up his slow circling and I was glad that I could be with him. In the morning, as I walked home to end my marriage, I felt as though I might have made a difference in the world. Never since has my life been any better.

ADVICE AND SANDWICHES

Pat O'Connor

Since 'Advice and Sandwiches' was published, Pat O'Connor has won the Seán Ó Faoláin Prize, been shortlisted for the Francis McManus Award and Fish Short Story Prize, longlisted for the Over the Edge New Writer of the Year Award and published in Southward, Crannóg, The Penny Dreadful, The Irish Independent *and* The Irish Times, *and anthologized and broadcast on RTÉ and 95FM. In 2014, he was a Writer in Residence in Tianjin, China.*

At lunchtime, Julie came out of Hodgeson & Co. and clattered down the steps into the street. She kept her face down so no one could see how choked-up she was. Her numbers were good, her clients commended her, she'd worked extra hours so long she couldn't remember any other way – yet she'd been passed-over for promotion again. Julie blinked furiously. It was like being clouted on the side of the head with a brick.

Normally she would bounce right back. It was her inheritance from her dad – he was always cheerful, always optimistic no matter what, to his very last breath. But that morning, Garry, her boyfriend – no, her ex-boyfriend – had announced he was leaving her, barely a month after suggesting they move in together. He said he'd met someone 'really exciting'. And he had that self-indulged look; he actually expected that she'd be delighted for him. And now this promotion thing. Swerving along the crowded sidewalk, Julie's face convulsed as she tried not to sob. In many aspects of her life she just didn't know which way was up. How could she bounce back when she didn't know which way was up?

She moved fast away from anywhere she might meet her colleagues, along the route she took to work each morning. A shop-space that had long been vacant was a buzz of activity. A voice was calling out, people were straining their necks and laughing. A sign over the opening said Advice and Sandwiches, and a placard said *Queue Here – Advice from $7 – Gourmet Sandwiches Free.* The queue was the shape of a U, with a rope on little white poles to keep order. A burst of laughter rose from the crowd; a good-natured sound. Julie strode past. There was a cheer and clapping. She took a quick, grudging glance. People were saying 'Aww' like they were affected by something. A sandy-haired man wandered dazedly out, holding a wrapped sandwich. People turned to watch him go; they nodded knowingly to one another, until laughter from inside made them turn, crane their necks to see. Julie walked on, and the laughter faded behind. Street sounds closed around her, everything was grey and worn and bare. Before the next intersection she wheeled around and went back. She joined the end of the queue.

She was too short to see what was happening. The queue was in three lines by now. A man's voice shouted 'Next!' and a woman called out some sort of enquiry. Julie couldn't quite catch what happened, but things seemed to be funny. A woman left the shop looking embarrassed and amused; she scuttled off, gripping her sandwich in both hands. Next to leave was a younger woman whose sandwich hung in her hand. She moved slowly, wide-eyed, like she might bump into things.

'Next!'

Julie was no longer the last, and neither could she see over the people in front. A male voice called out: 'I hate my job. What'll I do?'

'Either make it so you like it, or else live cheaper, build up cash, then resign and look for a job you do like. Seven dollars. What you want to eat?'

'Aah ... gimme a ham and cheese and tomato sandwich. No, a sub. A sub, please.'

'One ham, cheese, tomato sub. Look at that, ready already. How about that? Next!'

There was a low voice up the front.

'Can't hear you honey. A little louder.'

A woman's voice became shrill.

'My boyfriend's going to leave me and he only asked last month if I'd move in with him. What'm I gonna do?'

A murmur rippled around. Julie's skin froze. She waited with her mouth open.

'Honey, you might want to think – do you love him all over or do you just like the way he looks? If you love him, then give it your best shot and keep doing it, but if it's everything or nothing with him then it ain't you he's thinking of. Start over and just really enjoy your life, and love will come. That's seven dollars. What you want to eat?'

'Emm ... oh anything ...'

'Tuna lettuce tomato pannini. Green wrapper. Next!'

Someone behind Julie reminded her to move along. She jumped to close the gap.

Many of the customers couldn't say what they wanted to eat. If they delayed, the man giving the advice ordered for them. Nobody objected.

'My wife's a bitch. What'm I goin' to do about it?'

A cocky voice, his friends egging him on.

'Go and ask her forgiveness for your own shortcomings. That's ten dollars. What you wanna eat?'

'Hey, I thought it was seven dollars a sandwich!'

'Sandwiches are free – read the signs. Advice starts at seven dollars and goes up from there. You got the ten dollars?'

'Aah … yeah, OK.' The voice was contrite now. There was knowing laughter, some jeering.

'What you want then?'

'Ham and cheese … aah … with mustard and pickle. On white.'

'Ham, cheese, mustard, pickle on white!'

'Can I get the green wrapper?'

'Next!'

Everyone laughed outright. Julie didn't get the joke – people were too close-packed to see. She began to feel nervous. At the first bend in the queue, she saw notices on the wall.

Advice Average $7. Free sandwich with all advice
No advice, no sandwich
Green wrappers share lunch between two
No loitering at counter

A man wearing mirrored sunglasses was calling out the advice. He had three people behind him making the orders.

The line was moving at amazing speed. Julie began to fidget. A girl with frizzed hair and blue eye-shadow was waiting at the end of the counter. Julie thought it must be the girl whose boyfriend was leaving.

'Next!'

'Where's the best place to get a sandwich round here?'

A burst of laughter all around. It was a youngish man in a black pinstriped suit. He laughed too.

'Right here, sir. Only honest advice and honest ingredients. Seven dollars. What you want?'

'How about a BLT sub?'

'One BLT sub, side order barbeque oyster and crispy cress pannini. Cut all that in small slices, green wrapper and give it to that girl there. You OK with that?' – he asked the girl with the blue eye-shadow. She nodded, blankly. He turned to the pinstripe. 'You OK with that?'

The man looked taken aback, but he nodded. 'Sure, no problem.'

'OK young lady, you take the green wrapper and you give him one slice at a time, I got the feeling his mouth is wider than his neck.' Everyone laughed. The pinstripe hung his head in mock shame. 'We don't want him to choke, right?'

There was a cheer as the pair left with their green wrapper. Everyone moved along. Julie felt exhilarated and nervous. Coming to the final line, she barely heard the questions. People got fidgety, kneading their hands, hopping from foot to foot. Julie realised she was only three people from the end. She moved her elbows to cool herself. What would she ask? How quickly the remaining few were being served …

Julie was looking directly into the mirrored glasses. Her lip trembled. The man smiled.

'Is it about work?'

Julie nodded.

'Come right this way.'

He lifted the flap on the counter.

Julie mumbled: 'No no … that's not …'

But she tottered forward. What else could she do? The man took her handbag and put it in a cupboard.

'Wash your hands and make yourself a nice sandwich. Then get an apron and, well, start making the orders. OK?'

Julie nodded slowly. She made a roll from ingredients near her; roast beef and cold baked vegetables. The sandwich-maker at the end, a stout middle-aged man, slid tubs of mayonnaise and salad toward her. Julie smiled at him. She sat on a blue plastic crate. One of the other makers, a red-haired woman, gave Julie a cup of water and a smile in the easy stride of getting lettuce from a fridge.

Julie ate her roll like she was hovering over the scene. The sandwich-makers worked quickly but not hurriedly. They spent time getting things right. Julie finished her roll and sat looking. The man with the reflective glasses gave longer advice depending on how busy the sandwich-makers were, although one time he gave advice for so long all the makers became idle.

Julie went to the worktop. She found disposable gloves, a paper hat and an apron. Next time a sandwich of the ingredients near her was called, she made it and handed it to the sunglasses man. After that first sandwich, time rolled like honey from a jar. She made sandwich after sandwich in a daze.

'Next!'

'What's the best sandwich for someone who loves cats?'

'A shared sandwich. Seven dollars. What you want?'

'Oh? Emm … chicken, some salt, light mayo.'

'On plain?'

'Plain.'

'Chicken, some salt, light mayo on plain, green wrapper. Next!'

'Yeah, umm … how do I get to share lunch with that girl?'

'Bring flowers tomorrow, something small for her cats, and don't expect a thing in return. Maybe the day after you might get the green. Seven dollars, what'd you like?'

'Umm … chicken roll. Just chicken. Is there smoked chicken?'

'One smoked chicken roll …'.

'Emm … excuse me? Excuse me?'

'Yes, ma'am.'

'I don't mind, I mean … could that man get the green wrapper today?'

'Ma'am, you can ask anyone to join you any time you want, you don't have to ask me …'

'Yeah but … you know …'

'OK, make that smoked chicken roll in the green wrapper. Thank you. Next!'

A young man with a knapsack was next. His hair was shiny, curly at the sides. He looked dazzled.

'I'd like a… I don't know …'

'What advice d'you want?'

'Advice? Emm … what could I do that's kinda worthwhile, I guess?'

Everyone laughed. The young man looked around, bemused.

'Well, sir, so happens we have a vacancy coming up right here.'

Julie and the other makers looked up. There were only four spaces. They looked at one another to see who might be leaving. The counter-hatch was lifted and the young man came in just like Julie had done. He seemed happily bewildered. The man in the mirrored glasses smiled at the makers.

'Do any of you guys have sunglasses?'

The makers quickly shook their heads. Except Julie. She had sunglasses in her handbag. The man in the mirrored glasses looked directly at her. Julie felt a thickening in her throat. She had been enjoying herself so much. How long had she been there? She had been floating. Her dad used to say all things come to an end, there had to be an end so there could be a beginning. She looked at the new young man. He had beautiful eyes. She turned to the man in the mirrored glasses.

'I have sunglasses.'

'OK! So after this fella has himself a sandwich, if you give him your apron, that'd be great.'

Julie made sandwiches until the young man was finished eating. He stood, awkward and self-conscious, while she put her apron over his head. She told him how the making was organised, and it was astonishing how much she could tell him. Everyone beamed at them. His eyes were green and brown, and they were honest. When he was ready to make his first sandwich, she cupped his face in her hands and she kissed him. Julie barely heard the commotion. The man in the mirrored glasses said: 'OK, miss, let's see those glasses.'

Julie got her handbag. She took out the sunglasses. With sunglasses on, nobody would be able to see her eyes, and she was glad of that. It was a good idea. She said to the man in the mirrored glasses: 'I'd like to thank you. Really. It was great.'

'No, thank *you*, miss. We appreciate what you're doing.'

He reached out and she shook his hand. Then he lifted the hatch and he walked away past the queue. She stood staring after him, her hand still extended.

'Hey miss! What's the best stock on NASDAQ for a quick punt?'

Two young men in suits, jostling each other. They found the question hilarious. Julie gaped at them blankly. Then she said: 'Do you own the place you live in?'

'Me? Uuh … no?'

'Then you can't afford a punt on the NASDAQ. That's ten dollars. What do you want to eat?'

ANOTHER BREAKFAST WITH YOU

Máire T. Robinson

Máire T. Robinson lives and works in Dublin City. Since her story was published in New Irish Writing in The Irish Independent, *she has written two books: a short-story chapbook,* Your Mixtape Unravels My Heart *(2013) and a debut novel,* Skin, Paper, Stone, which *will be published by New Island Books this year.*

Love and hate are the same thing. I know that now. It's only the temperature that's different, like bread and toast, or cheddar and fondue. I would love if Malachy hated me; to know he lays awake at night fuming as my name reverberates in his head; that images of me flash into his mind unbidden, leaving scorch marks on his retina; that he shuffles about his house when nobody is home cursing me aloud to the sink, the table and chairs, the hardwood floor – *Fuckin' bitch . . . stupid fucking cunt* – that he tears out his black hair in clumpfuls from the sheer frustration of trying to contain his hatred of me. But he doesn't. I gave him no reason to. I know that now he feels nothing for me but the opposite of love, and the true opposite of love is not hate, but indifference.

After him, I was restless. I changed jobs. I changed hair colour. I changed city. After him, I was burned, cautious. I'd start seeing some fella and I'd worry he'd be just like Malachy. Then I'd end up disappointed when it turned out he wasn't. In Galway, I found work with a temp company like the one I'd worked for in Dublin. I got to know the outskirts of the city, the bus routes to the business parks, the different names of the endless roundabouts, the grey houses that lined the streets like crooked teeth. I answered phones and took messages and filed bits of paper, but it was different now. Before, my days had been filled with him, like a drug: waiting to see him, then seeing him, then thinking about having seen him. Now there was this void. I wondered how people knew what they were supposed to do with their lives. I could see it there, my life playing out in front of me, but it was like this foreign thing I couldn't get inside.

I heard someone say once that the break-up of a relationship is like a death that only two people experience. So I suppose you could say that I mourned when it was over, but he didn't. I saw the pictures of his engagement party in *Irish Society Magazine.* He was beaming, indecently gleeful. *Food columnist, Hannah Richardson, celebrates her engagement to Dublin barrister Malachy McNulty.* In the interview she said when they had met and the dates didn't add up. In the photos, he was wearing the cornflower-blue shirt I gave him for his birthday. The one I couldn't afford, but bought anyway because I knew the colour would bring out his eyes. And it did.

When I was made redundant, it didn't bother me at first. I thought I'd find some other office work like I always had in the past. But every day of the week people were losing their jobs. Businesses were closing down. A Burger King opened in Galway and a thousand people showed up for the open job interviews. It made the evening news. All these architects and teachers and accountants desperate for work: kids to feed, mortgages to pay.

At least I didn't have that to worry about. So, I sank into my unemployment like a relaxing bath. I wore pyjamas all day. I watched daytime TV. I drank. Sometimes I was filled with a giddy feeling of getting away with something, like when you'd be off sick from school and you could watch telly all day, and you'd laugh to yourself thinking of all the saps at their desks doing maths. But other times I was filled with fear, a paralysis that made leaving the flat impossible.

I was flicking channels one day, and there she was, Malachy's wife. *Home Cooking With Hannah.* She was wearing a floral apron and smiling at the camera as she sifted flour into a bowl. I realised that it wasn't some TV studio done up to look like a kitchen. It was their kitchen, in their farmhouse in County Wicklow. I recognised it from that magazine spread they did after their daughter was born. They were photographed in various rooms, all *restored faithfully using local materials.* I know I shouldn't have looked at it. I couldn't not look at it.

I could see why Hannah had been given her own TV show. She wasn't like those female chefs you see on British TV, food pornographers mugging for the cameras and describing everything as 'orgasmic'. She was natural and understated. I'd seen her photo before but never heard her voice. I liked the way her diction trilled with polished pronunciation. She sounded Irish, but not Irish. What you might call West-Brit if you felt like insulting her. Listening to her speak, you couldn't help but picture a childhood filled with pony rides, skiing trips, ballet recitals and various social engagements with the type of people who use 'summer' as a verb. The type of childhood Malachy also had, and now their children would have. I knew that *they* summered in Tuscany. She loved the bold rustic flavours of the region. She wrote about them in her first book, *Bold Rustic Flavours of Tuscany.*

I started watching Hannah's show every day. There was something reassuring about her, something indestructible. A toxic gas cloud could float over from Sellafield killing everything in its wake, making no allowances for school children or baby seals or high-ranking civil servants, and there she would be still baking scones in her Aga, an invisible force field of middle-class charm rendering her untouchable. After a few weeks, I even attempted some of the recipes. Sometimes she mentioned him and I imagined their life together.

'These freshly baked scones are just perfect for family get-togethers. They're a particular favourite of my husband's,' she said.

I used to cook breakfast for Malachy the odd time he stayed over. 'Don't you know how to cook anything other than eggs?' he said.

'Eggs are good for you. They contain protein.'

'So does steak.'

He never stuck around for long. Always work to do, or so he said, even at weekends. 'Your flat is always so fucking cold.'

'So come back to bed and I'll warm you up.'

'Be sure not to over-handle the dough as this can make the scones rubbery. Place them close together on the tray. This will encourage them to rise, not spread.' Hannah tapped the underside of the scones and they made a hollow sound. 'Perfect,' she said.

'Perfect,' I mimicked as I tipped out the burnt solid mass that hit the counter like a brick.

The day we found out our jobs were gone, everyone was talking on their phones, or crying, or crying into their phones. I felt stupid just standing there. I couldn't cry and I couldn't think of anyone to call so I rang the talking clock. *At the beep, the time will be 12.22. Beeeep.* Jim Fahy was at the gates with his RTÉ News microphone, asking people for their reactions.

'How are you feeling?' he asked me.

'Grand,' I said. I was thinking that he looked much taller than he does on telly. 'I mean, terrible. It's terrible. Sorry about that. I think I'm in shock.'

On the bus home I wondered what I'd look like on screen. Later, I watched the evening news but I hadn't made the cut. Instead, they used a clip of Gráinne from accounts. 'I don't know what I'm going to do!' she wailed into the camera lens. The light fell on her face, showing up the line of downy hair on her upper lip and the purplish shadows under her eyes that looked like bruises.

The more I watched Hannah's show, the more my cooking started to improve. I found myself getting up early, making shopping lists and scowering supermarket shelves for ingredients. I stopped spending my dole money on vodka and cigarettes and started buying things like pimento stuffed olives and vanilla pods. One day I went into town and enrolled on a cookery course. On my way home, I stopped into the newsagents. There was a picture of Malachy and Hannah on the front of one of the tabloids. 'TV Chef's Love-Rat Hubbie in Au-Pair Shocker' screamed the headline. I skimmed through the article, then bought a copy and headed home to read it properly.

Inside the newspaper, there were pictures of the au-pair alongside her 'exclusive story' of the affair. 'We liked to get steamy in the kitchen,' she was quoted as saying. Then at the end of the article, alongside a photo of her staring mournfully into the middle-distance: 'I still have feelings for Malachy.' The strange thing is, she looked just like Hannah, only a less polished version, like some second-rate actress who had been hired to play Hannah in one of those 'straight to DVD' biopics. It was as if Malachy had thought he wanted the new, but the familiar won out, like going abroad but drinking in an Irish bar. Maybe she was an act of rebellion, an antidote to all that perfection.

Every day, there were more and more revelations in the papers. I read them over coffee in my tiny kitchen, which felt different now, warmer, transformed by the daily smell of fresh baking. More women came forward with stories of their affairs with Malachy. There was speculation that Hannah would leave him, that she would cancel her forthcoming book tour. Still, she refused to be interviewed and never made a statement. There she was on TV every day as always.

'Perfect,' she said as she piled the almond and orange zest moon-shaped biscuits onto a floral serving tray. And they were perfect. And so was she, the chaos of the universe controlled in her measured stirring of the eggs and the way she sifted the flour just so.

When I told Malachy I was pregnant, he offered me money, said he'd take care of everything. I told myself he would change his mind. I waited. I pictured the new life we would have together, the three of us. Maybe I pictured this new life as something like those photos of him and Hannah in *Irish Society Magazine*. But then I stopped waiting because there was nothing to wait for any more.

'Maybe it's for the best,' he said. 'We had fun though, didn't we?' As if we'd been playing a game of pool and our hour was up. *Had.* Just like that.

I bought my copy of *Home Cooking With Hannah* and stood in line. I could see her smile and sign books for the people up ahead. I opened the book and looked inside. It was dedicated 'To My Darling Husband, Malachy'. I edged forward in the line. I wanted to tell her that we were the same. I wanted to kick over her display of books and spit in her face. I wanted her to see that we were not the same. I wanted to ask her which of his faces he showed to her and which of his faces were real. I wanted to tell her how tired it made me, hating somebody because they didn't love me. I wanted to ask if she was tired too. I wanted to take her hand and lead her out into the street to run and run in the rain until we were both out of breath and laughing like in a film.

I remembered then the feeling I had when me and Malachy were together, like I could never get close enough to him. I used to scrape my fingernails down his back to make him bleed, to claim him, but it was no good. Even with my arms around his neck, my mouth on his, our bodies entwined, we were too far apart.

'I want to open you up and crawl inside,' I told him and he gave me his lazy smile like he understood what I meant. But I don't know any more. When I picture it now, it looks more like a smirk. What I remember most is his mouth, and always the surprising coldness of his kiss.

At the top of the queue, Hannah smiled at me. 'Hi there, thanks for coming,' she said, reaching to take the book from my hands. 'Who will I make this out to?'

2012

SEPIA

Monica Corish

Monica Corish was shortlisted for the Hennessy Emerging Fiction Prize in 2012. Her first poetry collection, Slow Mysteries, *was published by Doghouse Books in 2012. She won the 2013 North West Words Poetry Prize, and is 2014/2015 SPARK Writer in Residence at the* Leitrim Observer. *She leads workshops in the North-West. www.monicacorish.ie*

I still have the photograph, of a man and a woman who were scarcely more than a boy and a girl. Frank is standing behind me in his brown suit, which I remember was brown, not made brown by the sepia fading of the photograph. His collar is buttoned high and I am wearing a high-necked striped work blouse, tucked in to my high-waisted skirt. The look on his face is so proud – I remember that look – and his right hand is resting on my left shoulder. Sweet God in Heaven, I remember that moment.

I had met Frank the autumn before the travelling photographer came to the island, one lunchtime when I was working in Mrs Ring's post office shop in Knightstown. I used to fill in there for an hour every day. My mother liked the arrangement, because I was in the village most days anyway, to buy messages or to sell eggs. And because, instead of paying me, Mrs Ring let us buy from the shop at cost price.

On the first day we exchanged only the words of business, but I remember noticing his accent, and his astonishing fair hair, only a few shades darker than white. No one on our island had hair that colour, the same colour as the fine, pale sand on Beiginis where I used to swim as a girl. The rest of that week he came in every day, at lunchtime, to get matches, candles, to buy stamps, to post letters to his family. I noticed the unusual surname on the envelopes, Corish, and the addresses, scattered all around the rim of Ireland. I knew by then that he was a lightkeeper out on Tearaght, so I supposed his people were in the same business. And then, all of a sudden, he was gone.

And then he was back, six weeks to the day he left, into the shop looking for stamps for his letters home, and again the next day, for matches. Mrs Ring came in just as he was leaving and muttered about how that boy must have a sieve for a brain, the way he's in here every day looking for something or other, but she was smiling into the till as she said it.

And so it went on, our gentle, unspoken courtship, broken by his six weeks away on Inis Tearaght, resumed on his one week of return. I cannot remember a single thing we talked about, only that my heart lifted when he walked into the shop, and missed him when he wasn't there. I don't know why he didn't ask me to walk out with him. Maybe he was simply shy, as I was shy. I don't know. Whatever the reason, we continued as we were, both knowing but neither speaking of the growing warmth that moved between us.

And then the travelling photographer came to the island and set up his wares in the lobby of the Royal Hotel, across the road from Mrs Ring's, where I could see all the comings and the goings and the excitement. He gathered all the spider plants from the windowsills into one place, so that we, the windswept residents of Valentia, looked like we lived on a tropical island. And he covered a section of the crimson-flocked wallpaper with a pale silk sheet that I longed to touch, the same colour as Frank's hair.

It was one of Frank's weeks of shore relief, and he came into the shop with a fierce and serious look in his eye. I remember wondering what ailed him. And then he said it, bluntly: *Will you have your photograph taken with me?* I felt a rush of blood that spread from my toes to the crown of my head. And I, shy careful I, said *Yes.* Just like that. *I'll be finished here in ten more minutes. I'll meet you then, inside the hotel.* And he smiled like a lighthouse.

I wanted to go home and change into my Sunday clothes, but I knew that if I did I'd never get out again. The photographer arranged us, me sitting in a straight-backed chair, Frank standing behind me and to my left. The photographer had already put his head beneath the black hood of the camera when I felt Frank's hand on my shoulder, light but burning through the fabric of my summer blouse. I think I may have stopped breathing. And then the photographer's voice saying: *Hold it,* and the very bright flash. Frank left his hand there for one second longer, then lifted it away. I turned around to look at him, and now my smile was like a lighthouse. But what I said was *I must go home now. I will see you tomorrow.* And he nodded, yes, and turned to pay.

My mother had heard by the time I got home, I had had my photograph taken with the young lighthouse keeper. It was an island, what did I expect? The wonder was that she hadn't heard before. News travels faster than footsteps here, no one knows how, only that it does. I remember what she said: *Don't go developing a* ghrá *for him. Just don't do it, girl. There's no use to it, we need you here. You can't marry a keeper and help on the farm and mind your father, and me when I need minding, for all that it's a well-heeled job. They are travelling men, for all their uniforms and their pensions, and you cannot be a travelling wife. So let that be an end to it.*

I remember how she turned from me then, her lips closed tight as a trap, to fill the kettle and stoke the range. And I said nothing. I had never learned to fight, and I knew I couldn't fight them on my own. I might have been able to do it if he had been by my side. But he would be gone most of the time, out on Tearaght six weeks or more, or gone completely, transferred to some far-flung corner of Ireland. And for all the strength of the lightkeeper's dwellings that ran along the seafront in Knightstown, for all that they stood for and how excellent the world would consider the match, I knew it wasn't enough. It wasn't enough to make me strong in the face of my father's illness and my mother's need, and the grim straight line of her mouth.

The next day he came into the shop with the photograph in one hand and an open letter in the other. I took the photograph, but I looked at the letter. I skimmed: *Dear Mr Corish, the Commissioners are pleased to inform you . . . following your successful . . . urgent need . . . your effects will be forwarded . . .* I skimmed until my eyes tripped over the words *Aran Island South.* It was a world away. I looked up at him then and he said *Marry me.* But I shook my head, *No, I can't. They won't let me go.* And he said, with all the sureness of a young man, *They will. They will. I will persuade them.*

I agreed to let him walk out to the farm with me, the whole island watching, although I knew it would do no good. My mother greeted him with a terrible politeness. My father sat with his two canes and his useless legs in his chair by the fire. I sat outside, on the bench under the window, waiting. And Frank sat with a tiny porcelain cup in his hand, juggling cake and plate and spoon and sugar and saucer. I didn't hear him ask the question – he had a quiet voice at the best of times – but I heard her answer: *No . . . I am sure you understand . . . under other circumstances . . . it will work out for the best . . . you are both young . . .* And I heard my father's silence. Then there was Frank's voice again, a second time, and a third. After the third *No* he rose and shook their hands and walked out the door, and we walked together down the lane to the road. I put my arm through his, knowing she was watching. It was my one and only rebellion. When we had passed the hawthorn tree and had come to the gate, hidden from the house, he turned and kissed me. It was the sweetest moment of my life.

Then he walked on, alone, back to the village, and I returned to the house. The back door was open – she had gone out, to the haggard for turf. As I reached to get my apron my father took my left hand in his and kissed it and said, *I am sorry*. Then she came back in and began to feed the fire, and I turned to peel the potatoes, and nothing more was said.

I went to Mrs Ring's shop the next day – I thought about not going, but I could not bear the house – and he came into the shop as before, buying provisions for his great journey to the north, and now we were like two kind strangers to each other. And so it was for the rest of the week, with the island watching.

The ferry was already waiting down at the pier when he came in on the last day. Mrs O'Connell was in the shop, buying flour, but when she saw Frank she made some excuse and left. He took my two hands in his across the counter and said *I will not forget* and I said *We have the photograph*, and then he squeezed my hands and was gone. Although it was the lunch hour, Mrs Ring came into the shop to watch with me. She put her hand against my lower back and held it there as the ferry pulled away from the pier, and all the people on board became smaller and smaller, until I couldn't see their faces anymore.

And then, after fifty-nine years, I heard his name again, last week. I had driven into the village to buy stamps when I overheard two fishermen talking about a new banker who had arrived in Cahirciveen, the market town on the mainland. *Corish*. Apart from that one Labour Party politician, it was a name I hadn't heard spoken since Frank had left the island. So I drove home and took down my hat from the box over the wardrobe, and put on my good coat, and drove back into Knightstown to catch the ferry to the mainland, and then the bus into the town.

It wasn't my bank – my family had always used the other bank in the town – but I went in anyway and told the porter that I wished to speak to the manager. I wasn't waiting more than two minutes when a tall fair man came toward me, so like Frank I nearly said his name. He brought me into his office and said, after the usual pleasantries about the weather:

– *So, Mrs O'Sullivan, what can I do for you?*
– *It's Miss O'Sullivan,* I said. *Miss. Your name,* I said. *I heard your name. It's not usual around here.*
– *That's true,* he said. *It's a Wexford name. It's common enough in that part of the country.*
– *I was wondering, were you anything to a Frank Corish, a lighthouse keeper?*
– *Why yes,* he said. *He was my uncle. But he died a few years ago. You knew him?*
– *I did. It was a long time ago, long before you were born. It was when he was stationed out on Tearaght. And tell me, did he ever marry?*
– *No,* he said. *He never married. He smiled at some memory. Frank would have made a fine father. He was a good uncle to us. He was a good man.*
– *He was,* I said. *He was a lovely man.*

HOMO SPIRITUALIS

Carmel McMahon

Carmel McMahon grew up in Ashbourne, County Meath. She lives in New York City and attended NYU and CCNY, where she was awarded the Mack Graduated Prize for writing. Since 'Homo Spiritualis' was shortlisted for a Hennessy Award, she has been working on a book of creative non-fiction.

It was my first real job in NYC. Personal Assistant to a wealthy woman on the Upper East Side. It took a while for me to train her to call me her assistant rather than her secretary and it took a while for me to learn that I was not being paid for my opinion. It had been a slow crawl out of the waitressing game, but I landed an assistantship at a New York museum, unaware that positions of this sort, while miserably paid, are usually reserved for Ivy-educated daughters until they find a husband – not for a broke Irish immigrant with anxiety issues and drink problems.

I liked to imagine I was maintaining a veneer of normalcy, but then I would accidentally wear my shirt inside out, or absentmindedly email something inappropriate to the entire museum, or spend the day hiding behind my monitor, praying for relief from yet another wretched hangover and vowing never to drink again. Or worst of all, I would burst into tears for no reason, other than the fact that my unconscious mind had kicked up some mundane memory from the past, like the time I stood with school friends at dusk, in one of the newer housing estates of Ashbourne in County Meath; we were laughing while the dying light played red and gold notes across our faces and hair. Why the laughter? Why the pristine preservation of this isolated fragment? And why now, to feel it viscerally twenty years later? To feel this disconnected part of myself scramble to figure out how it fits into this life. Then to feel, more forcefully, the absolute futility of being. How could I not drink?

So, while my behaviour was never the stuff of dismissals, I sensed a talking-to was in the offing. I would never have survived the embarrassment. I knew, that they knew, that my mind had emigrated with a bottle of whiskey and what showed up was the derelict and dishevelled body it had once inhabited. I had no choice but to quit.

The new job came in the nick of time. The big house was a balm for my troubled soul. The objects were beautiful. Beauty beyond intellect, beyond argument. My boss, a life-long collector, had a reputation for having a great eye. She flipped through the auction house catalogues, stopping at the pieces that fit the aesthetic she had cultivated from childhood; from within herself, impervious to outside influence or market tastes. She never attempted to articulate the meaning of an object; she didn't have to, as my set did, aimlessly flapping about trying to pin our opinions on air. Her housekeeper was a kind and gentle Haitian woman whose presence calmed every frenetic object it touched. Then there was Mlle. Georgette Moreau ....

New York has an abundance of these women. Keen-eyed and ancient with impeccable style from the overall effect of their manner to the smallest detail of their dress. Georgette's job was Fashion Advisor to my boss, a position wherein she yay'd and nay'd the offerings of French and Italian couturiers. I was fascinated. She, however, made no effort to hide the fact that she did not like the cut of my jib. And so our relationship began.

Every day I offered to make her a cup of tea and every day she refused. There was a certain cup, a level for the water, the length of time a tea bag should steep. A complicated procedure. Certainly too much for a clumsy, distracted people-pleaser to cope with.

Six months passed when she began to open up to me in the form of a rant. Every day she carried the tale of some dissatisfaction she had encountered on the way to work. It usually began with the bus driver. He drove too fast, he drove too slow, he allowed too many people on the bus, he did not respond when she said hello. A sure sign that the end days were upon us when small civilities were so readily dispensed with. Some man at the bank, a cyclist, a traffic light, a pothole, a tourist, a dog, etc. Then for the rest of the day the events of her life would be filtered through the lens of that dissatisfaction. My stock response was a sympathetic 'Hmm, hmm,' for I could certainly relate to the difficulties of existing alongside others when I am always in the right.

Whenever she mentioned war-time France, Georgette had my full attention. These few years had shaped the being who sat before me today halfway across this world of time and space. 'People did not groom their dogs in France during the war,' she would say. 'They did not waste their pennies on such frivolities as bows and booties for their pets, they did not bend down to pick up their shit! People who have dogs in the city are sick. Selfish, sick people!'

She also started to accept a cup of tea. She directed me in the making of it, as the English *Directrice* of her primary school had directed her. 'The English,' she would say, 'know how to make a cup of tea.' Hmm. The Irish, I happen to know, make it better. It is an old argument, each accusing the other of making weak, sugary tea. A direct reflection, no doubt, of a moral flaw in the character. But I make no mention. She accepts a biscuit only if it is made with real sugar and real butter. These she nibbles for an achingly long time, as if to make them last. What memories, I wonder, lurk there beneath the layers of Chanel, Vuitton, Hermès?

She developed a pain in her leg, which her doctor put down to age. It prevented her from taking her daily walk home across Central Park. She began to limp in an exaggerated fashion to match her increasingly cantankerous moods. Some days she would drag her foot behind her and mutter curses in French and stubbornly refuse my insistent offers to help.

Increased absences forced my boss to address the situation. 'Perhaps it is time to retire, Gigi?' she tentatively put forth to the eighty-year-old woman. The following day Georgette entered in a particularly beautiful camel hair coat and a pale pink pashmina. Her cropped silver-grey locks were spiked just enough to betray her punk-rock heart. 'I know when I am not wanted!' she yelled, as she threw her keys down. 'I quit!' Then she turned around and hobbled out. My heart sank. The Haitian woman could not eat for days, and my boss took to her bed.

I missed the old woman telling the same stories over and over, like some soothing steadiness in my fraying life. Not the words themselves, because I had long ceased listening, but the surety of the cadence, of knowing how each episode would play out: the way her brother would berate her for dipping her bread in her soup. Just because they were poor, did not mean they had to act like peasants. The apple tree in her mother's garden from which jams and jellies were made. That there was no obesity then, for the people ate what they needed and walked because they had to.

I took to visiting her the odd evening. She lived with a fat, furry cat in a rent-controlled apartment on the Upper West

Side. The kind of place that New Yorkers die for. Someone told me that people allude to real estate at least once day in the city because it is such a limited resource. My own one room being only slightly larger than the bathroom in my parents' house. Georgette loves having me over. She dresses for the occasion, and I take care on those days to wear something I think she will approve of. Usually one of my many Givenchy-inspired vintage dresses, which she will briefly admire then give me in-depth instructions on how to deal with the tiny rip or stain in the fabric. I bring cheese and bread. The table is always laid for tea with mis-matched cups and saucers. There is always a bowl of cherries and a plate of chocolates. The teapot, she always tells me, is from a flea market upstate.

She begins to speak of her first years in the US. Of the time she worked for a young English woman in Florida who had married a wealthy old man for his money. When they divorced, the woman moved to New York. She bought a tiny studio on Central Park South, and she drank herself to death in it. Of the time she worked as a cook for Woody Allen, a sweet and simple man, who invited her to use his apartment before she found one of her own. More stories! I demanded, drunk on Earl Grey and Petit Écolier. I felt something in those days with that old woman that I had not felt before in my life. It was this: that sitting in her apartment with her prattling on, and the cat, and the tea, and the evening sun, that I was, in those moments, exactly where I was meant to be.

As the months continued their steady march on, I became aware of the descent of her mind and her movement. She had begun to answer the door in her dressing gown. Once she told me about her previous cat, Melou, who had passed away. Georgette had taken her ashes into Central Park and scattered them over Strawberry Fields. I asked her when it was that Melou died; she turned around to face a framed painting of a black and white cat. 'Melou,' she asked it, 'when did you die?' Then she turned back to me and replied, 'She says fifteen years ago.' Whenever I left after that, she held on to me when I hugged her goodbye, and I had the feeling that I was holding a little child. I gently rubbed her hollow, papery back and promised to return soon.

One afternoon I called to make a tea date. The phone rang and rang. A few days later I called again, and again, no answer. I went to her building and the doorman told me that Georgette had fallen, and that she had been found where she lay, babbling and incoherent in a pool of her own urine. She was taken to the hospital, and then on to a nursing home on the Upper East Side.

The lobby of the nursing home is set up with seating arrangements for guests. Though there are none. The receptionist barely acknowledges my presence and omits telling me that the elevator is out of service, so I sit on an oilcloth-covered sofa for twenty minutes watching the light travel up and down but never stopping on the ground floor. There is a lonely feeling here. Not any more lonely than the loneliness that is always present everywhere, but here there is less of an effort to disguise it. Finally, I take the stairs. Good to keep the body moving, I think, to comfort myself.

I find Georgette slowly making her way in a walker down the peach/pink corridor. She is barely recognizable. Her hair and nails are long and unkempt. The stained green nightdress does not belong to her, and a pair of mismatched socks bunch around her ankles. She is a wisp of a thing now, but her eyes are clear and bright and sparkle with a new light. We *putz* on together very slowly, and she introduces me to her new Polish friend. A pretty, young blonde aide. 'I gant geep up wit dis one speeding about,' the blonde says. We small-talk awhile, and we laugh at ourselves in an easy way, we three European women, we three rebels who left kith and kin to end up here together on this day in April, in this year of Our Lord, 2011!

Georgette and I walk on. 'I have been here so long,' she tells me, 'that I have no memory of my life outside this place.' It has only been a week, I think to myself, but perhaps it is just as well. 'My mind is lucid for what is in front of my face and my memories of Burgundy,' she says, 'but everything else is gone.'

When visiting hours are over, she walks me to the door. 'It's not so bad,' she says. 'I just take it a day at a time, and today is a very good day, because you are here …' I held her for a long time, for what I knew would be the last time, and I felt the healing begin within me of a very deep wound, that I didn't even know was there.

2013

LAST BREATH

Brendan McLoughlin

Brendan McLoughlin was born in 1991 and grew up in Howth, County Dublin. He holds a BA in Economics, Politics and Law from DCU and an MA in Creative Writing from Queen's University, Belfast. 'Last Breath' – his first published story – won the 2013 Hennessy Writer of the Year Award. He has recently commenced study towards a PhD at Queen's, and has been awarded a bursary from the Arts Council of Northern Ireland.

Ailbhe watches as the new patient is brought in from the cold. The wheelchair screeches against the tiled floor of reception and everyone has a moment to breathe. She will be well looked after here, she can stop fighting now.

'Good morning.'

'It is,' replies the new patient.

'I'm Ailbhe. I'm a nurse on your ward. Let's go get you settled.'

'Thank you.'

She is placed in a large open-planned room with two other women. They have a view of the Dublin Mountains, but this is more for their visitors to occupy themselves with. It is hard for them most of all, the ones who must live on. She is lucky, this one, if she were a man she'd still be on that waiting list. Ailbhe thinks about all this as she inserts the morphine drip into the new patient's arm.

A family member comes over and pulls Ailbhe aside. 'How long does she have?'

'It's hard to say, everyone is different.'

'Should I tell the children to come home?'

'Oh, I think she has a few more days left in her. I'll let you know when the time is near.'

'Thanks, I'm Orla by the way, the sister.'

'This must be hard for you.'

'I'm not the one who's dying,' she says and pats Ailbhe on the arm before sitting down beside the bed and lifting a cup to the new patient's lips, holding it there until it is empty. Ailbhe watches and is certain that there is still some time. They are normally not thirsty towards the end.

Nursing: it is a profession that cannot facilitate the weak. Friends and family all tell her what an angel she is. *Ah sure I couldn't do it myself. It's a vocation. You couldn't not do it, sure you couldn't?*

Teaching: that's the route she almost found herself wandering down. A slower turnaround and far fewer deaths, at least that's what you hope. But she loves her job, can't see herself being anywhere else, doing anything else.

She walks down the corridor towards reception and smiles as she passes the smoking room. Tom, the lung cancer patient, sits at the table with a cigarette in one hand and his drip towering above him on a metal trolley. It is important that the patients feel like they can ask for anything. Let them have a cigarette inside if that's what they want, they've already been handed down the toughest punishment of all. When they no longer have the strength to get up, their beds are wheeled out onto the veranda where they can smoke in peace. *It is the little mercies,* she thinks. *These are what are provided here.*

They don't normally admit children, but very occasionally an exception will be made. Ailbhe stops outside the small private room and looks in through the window. The child can't be much older than ten or eleven. Teddy bears litter the foot of the bed, posters of actors and boybands cover the walls. The child looks so pale and her eyes are closed to the world. Dying is an exhausting process, the body uses up so much energy as it shuts itself down.

The girl's father looks on as the resident Capuchin, Brother Michael, places a hand gently against her face. This is not supposed to happen. Parents are not supposed to watch their children die.

Ailbhe feels a presence behind her. The girl's mother has been watching her watching them. She steps out of the way and nods politely to this woman who looks so tired.

'She's not going to wake up again, is she?'

'The pain relief is very strong.'

'She's only nine. I want to help her.'

'You're giving her exactly what she needs. You're letting her go.'

The girl's mother composes herself and goes into the room. Brother Michael comes out and closes the door behind him.

'I've given her the Sacrament of the Sick. She's going to sleep now.'

Ailbhe does not respond. She is aware that this man knows more about the patients here than anyone else. He spends his days walking from room to room, nodding at families and staff and when he thinks that death is imminent he will place a hand on the patients' faces and pray for them.

Ailbhe is working a double shift, won't be leaving until morning. She sits down on one of the many couches scattered across this warren of a hospice – so many alcoves and corridors. She slips off her shoes. Her feet are released and the pressure dissipates. People come and go, some alone, others in groups, all looking drained. The dying seem to float between life and death. They take on a new state, a new shape, those who dance along the precipice of this world and the next.

She looks at her watch and stands up, fixes herself by smoothing out her uniform with her hands and goes about her job: drips need to be replaced; medication has be divvied out; the morphine levels must be monitored.

She returns to the new patient. A woman sits beside the bed, but is not the sister, Orla. She is old, and this old woman holds the new patient's hand and whispers in her ear. Ailbhe realises that it does not get easier, no matter what age you are, no matter the age of your child: you will never be able to prepare yourself.

The old woman kisses the new patient on the cheek and squeezes her hand. 'God Bless.'

Ailbhe walks her out to the entrance, content with the silence between them as they make their way down the long corridor to reception.

'You're welcome to visit any time, day or night,' she says.

'Thanks. Do you know I have to force myself to get out of bed in the morning? I do it because she wouldn't want me to let it take over. She'd want me to get on with things.'

'She would.'

'I spoke to a nun yesterday. She told me that grief was the price we paid for loving others. I felt like shouting at her but I know all she was trying to do was help. It's easy for her, with God as her one love. Now you get back in there and look after my girl.'

Like a magician, the old woman produces a wad of tissue from the sleeve of her coat and blows her nose. She turns around and walks up the driveway towards the stone pillars at the entrance. Ailbhe does not move until the old woman reaches the main road and disappears out of sight.

They have had a good week, if you could call it that. Only one death: the woman who freed up the bed for the new patient. The mortuary, that cold place in the basement, is empty. The body was taken home immediately to be waked. It is cold, in the basement, but it is nothing like a hospital morgue. They are brought down in their beds, and look like they are sleeping. Each body is placed in a private room, with flowers and a Sacred Heart glowing in the corner. A book of condolence is left open on a small bedside table. The families can grieve in private here, and can spend as much time with their loved one as they wish.

She eats her dinner in the canteen, then goes back up to the ward to check on the new patient and is surprised by what she sees. There has already been a major change. The new patient coughs a horrible cough, the kind only those close to death can produce. Ailbhe fills a basin with warm soapy water and washes her.

'I'm so relieved.'

Then a cough.

'Are you in any pain?'

'No.'

She washes the arms, then the legs, the face. She goes to unbutton the pyjama top but she is stopped by a surprisingly forceful hand.

'I think you've done enough, thanks.'

Ailbhe has read the file. The new patient's stomach is heavily distended and she must be embarrassed by the fact that she looks pregnant. She refastens the buttons which have already been opened and smoothes out the bedclothes. There will be no new life brought into the world here.

'You don't look very comfortable.'

'It's just I had one of those air mattresses in the hospital, that's all.'

'We'll sort that now.'

She waits until the porters bring in the replacement bed. The new patient is transferred and when she closes her eyes Ailbhe leaves to find the staff bedroom. They will wake her if she is needed.

The alarm goes off. It is early. She washes her face and puts on her uniform. She did not sleep well, never does here. She always feels like a patient and imagines herself to be dying.

When she goes up to the ward, her heart sinks. The new patient is finding it hard to breathe and Brother Michael has a hand against her face as he prays. The time has come. Ailbhe goes to the nurse's station and looks up the next of kin. The phone rings and rings, and then an answer.

'Hello, Orla? This is the nurse from the hospice, we spoke briefly yesterday.'

'Is everything OK?'

'I think you should come in as soon as you can.'

'I'm on my way.'

Brother Michael leaves. Ailbhe sits beside the new patient and holds her hand. She talks to her, tells her that her family are coming, that she doesn't need to worry about anything, that it's alright for her to let go, and it all happens so quickly. The new patient's breathing becomes more laboured, less frequent. Then she is gone.

Ailbhe stands up and closes the dead patient's eyes, fixes her long blonde hair and places her hands by her sides. When she looks up she sees Orla standing in the doorway.

'I'm so sorry.'

Orla comes over to the bed and touches the dead patient.

A nervous laugh. 'Jesus, Cara. Could you not have waited for me?' Turning to Ailbhe, she says, 'You know she'd kill me for saying this, but I can't remember the last time she looked this good. She looks so peaceful.'

'They do say that we come back into ourselves after we die. All the pain is gone. If you need anything, I'll be over there.'

She turns her back on Orla and blesses herself. She goes over to the nurse's station and finds the waiting list. She scrolls her finger down the sheet of names, stops at the first woman and dials the number to let them know that there is a vacancy.

Her shift is over. She steps outside and breathes in the morning. Death is no stranger to this nurse, and Ailbhe knows that we cannot escape our own mortality. She makes her way up to the main road and stands at the bus stop.

When the bus pulls up and the door opens, warm air rushes out and hits her in the face, and for a brief moment she can almost feel Brother Michael's hand being pressed against her forehead.

IS THIS AUSTRALIA?

Sean Kenny

'Is This Australia?' was published in New Irish Writing in The Irish Independent *in 2013. Since then Sean Kenny has been a prize-winner in RTÉ's Francis MacManus Short Story Competition. His story, 'Ending It', was broadcast on RTÉ Radio 1. In 2014 he received the Hennessy Emerging Fiction Award.*

'Don't be too shocked, OK?'

I'm barely a step through the sliding door at Arrivals and Ciara's charging me down. Like I'm the one-millionth customer or something. Big oxygen-depriving hug and a face full of pearlies. And a whisper.

Don't be too shocked.

Well, OK. Because I'm flight-fuzzy, just off the deep vein thrombosis express from Sydney to Dublin. So just what it is I am supposed not to be shocked by, or at least not to display my shock at, is hazy.

Then I see Dad. But he doesn't seem to see me. Even after his eyes have locked on me. And I know.

'Hi, Dad.'

'Hello.'

'He wanted to be here,' says Ciara on the way to the car park. Which is funny, since he doesn't seem to know who I am. It explains why Ciara has been there every time I've Skyped him over the last while.

Not that I Skype him that often.

She was there, though, to the left of the screen the last time, holding his arm and repeating my questions. You know Skype. You don't know whether it's a poor connection or his hearing aid's acting up or it's terminal mental deterioration or what.

I mean, Ciara said things. By not saying things. The little evasions. 'He's having a great day today.' 'Yesterday evening he was so lucid.' 'At dinner on Sunday he was chatting to Jim about the football. Couldn't shut him up, throwing players' names out like confetti, he was.'

But still.

So we're on the M50, whizzing south past the big box units, and Ciara's doing the cheery *welcome home, great to see you* routine. And Dad's doing this zombie stare out the window. And a part of me wants to slap Ciara because it feels like I've been chucked in the deep end whilst she's just walking past whistling fucking 'Heigh-Ho'.

We arrive at Ciara's house. I make cursory small-talk with her husband, Jim. ('G'day, mate! How them Sheilas treatin' ye Down Under?' He's a gifted comic, is Jim.) We sit to eat dinner. I try not to stare as, supervised by Ciara, Dad shuffles forwards and lands rather than sits on his seat.

Jim is just saying what he'd like to do – or contract others to do – to Angela Merkel when there is an odd sound, somewhere between a cough and a shout. Dad is hammering the table with surprising vigour. Ciara is first to react, darting round to him and performing a rudimentary Heimlich manoeuvre. A king prawn plops onto Dad's lap.

'Fish!' he yells, flapping his arms. 'Fish! Fish! Fish! Fish!' I have never seen him as demonstrably upset in my life. Terror has seized his every sinew and is flailing him about like a puppet. He knocks the water from his glass, swipes his plate to the floor. Jim fails completely to hide his alarm, torn between compulsive staring and studious examination of his plate. I'm disturbed beyond movement or speech.

'It's OK now, Dad,' soothes Ciara, removing the prawn with a napkin. 'It's OK.'

'Fish,' says Dad, in a sort of whimper, like that of a small wounded animal. 'Fish.' Ciara strokes his head.

The rest of the meal passes with uneasy bursts of conversation, spikes of nervous laughter and troughs of silence.

I find an excuse to speak alone with Ciara by offering to help clean up.

'Do you like the new colour on the walls?' she asks. Why won't she stop smiling?

'Jesus, Ciara. Why didn't you tell me?'

'It was only done a few weeks ago. I didn't think you'd be *that* interested.'

'Just stop, OK? Dad. I'm talking about Dad.' She has a right old swig of Merlot.

'This is a bad day, OK? He has a lot … some, some really good days. I suppose I was hoping … just while you were here …' There's a trickle of a mascara-black tear down her cheek.

'Oh, Christ. I'm sorry. I thought …'

I realise I'm not sure what I thought. That she was hiding his deterioration from me so she could hog the role of dutiful child? That she'd think I couldn't handle it?

I'm thinking again about the last few Skype conversations. Dad was tired, said Ciara, or had a bad head-cold. I wanted to believe it. The calls lasted, what, two minutes? I was somewhere sunny and in love with Mandy and Dad's health was easily pigeonholed in a nicely remote corner of my brain. Filed neatly away with Death, The Meaning of It All and the rest of the existential-panic-of-the-4 a.m. insomniac gang. And I've been sleeping well lately.

But Ciara *was* hiding it. I feel the crackle and rise of anger and I'm breathing it out on her.

'Look, I'm sure it's been hard for you. But you didn't have the right to keep it from me.' Even as I speak I know it's projection. (Yeah, that's six months of therapy right there.) *You didn't have the right.* I sound like I'm in a fucking soap opera.

'OK, maybe I should have told you. I was just trying not to burden you with it. What could you do from Australia anyway? Look, I was going to tell you when …'

'When? When he died?'

'Jesus, Mark!' The volume has been rising but this is a scream of horror-movie pitch and volume.

Jim's head appears round the door.

'Everything all right in here?'

'It's fine!' shouts Ciara. Jim leaves.

There's a slow heavy settling in the kitchen. She rests her head on the kitchen counter, trailing tears. I hug her. She hugs me back. A little too tightly and for a little too long. *Clings* is the word. It feels like she's clinging to me. Like there's been a shipwreck and I'm a rock. I pull away.

'It's been pretty tough. It'd be great if you could help with him a little while you're here. Do you think you can manage?' Of course I don't think I can manage. Somebody appears to have removed my father's mind and sent it tumbling through several million heavy spin-cycles, before carefully reinserting it into his cranium. Then I look at Ciara at the sink, the slump of her, the purple hammocks slung under her eyes, the smile she's hoisting like a heavy flag.

'Of course. I'll do whatever I can.'

We're drinking coffee when Dad asks Ciara where his bedroom is.

'No, Dad. You're not staying with us tonight. Mark's here now. He's staying in your house with you.'

'Mark?'

Ciara is about to speak, then restrains herself. She catches Dad's eye and places a hand on my shoulder.

'Dad, you know Mark!'

'Mark,' says Dad.

It's weird being back in the house. Everything seems coated in a thin layer of must, like cheese slightly turned. It's possible that my mind may be sending the signal to my nose, though, rather than vice versa. Does Dad even live here any more, I wonder. In any case his slippers and pyjamas are present in his room. He sits on the bed and looks up expectantly at me like a child.

So, I crouch and untie his shoes and remove his socks.

'You can manage the rest yourself, can't you?'

He plucks at his trouser leg. OK, the trousers, then.

I unclothe the chalky wattled legs and it's impossible not to touch his skin. I'm a little repulsed and then repulsed by myself for being repulsed. I work through the garments, leaving his underpants till last. I uncover the pale droop of chest and stomach and the shrivelled hang of genitals. The awkwardness is all mine, and this is unsettling. Dad has reached some black oblivion beyond bodily prudery but it does not seem like a freedom.

I'm tucking him into bed. This is the natural cycle, right, the once cared-for returning the favour to the caregivers of their childhood. Except that Dad never did any tucking-in. Strictly Mam's role, God rest her, the tucking-in, the application of plasters and later the post-breakup tea-and-sympathising. Dad went out and worked and brought custard slices home on Fridays. He embraced me once, after I won a gold medal for a 50-metre breaststroke at a swimming gala. He quickly hooked an arm around my back whilst the other arm hovered tentatively, like a nervous cat unsure if it can make a jump, unable to quite complete the hug.

'Goodnight,' I say but there is no response.

I go down to the living room to watch the most mindless television I can find. There is a horrifically compulsive show called *Tallafornia*. My brain is sludgy with fatigue. I sink into a sitting sleep.

I'm awoken some time later by muffled sounds from above. I climb the stairs of my childhood.

In his room, Dad appears to be shouting at his socks.

'Bloody things,' he's saying, and I notice he's out of breath and weeping slightly, 'they're not working.'

'It's OK, Dad.' What else can you say? It plainly is not OK, as my father has been reduced to tears by hosiery. I manoeuvre his socks on and am surprised by the robustness of his feet, as though they too should be crumbling in concert with his mind.

'Time for breakfast?' he asks.

It's 2.42 a.m. 'Not really. Do you want to go back to sleep?'

He shakes his head.

'Why don't we go downstairs and watch some TV for a while?'

There's a screening of a Liverpool v. Manchester United match from 1994 on TV. It's a famous game, a dramatic 3–3 draw. We watched it together when I was a teenager, in this very room. I'm about to ask Dad if he remembers the game. Then I stop myself. Maybe I'm learning.

After some time he speaks.

'You're Mark,' he says to me and it feels, crazily, like I've just got a gold star from teacher. Earned recognition. I feel the stretch of the first true smile across my face since arriving home.

'That's right. Your son.'

'Son?'

'Yes. I live in Australia now.'

'Is this Australia?'

'No, this is Ireland. I'm here for a holiday.'

'Why would you go to Ireland for a holiday?'

'I came to see you. And Ciara, and some other people.'

'Who's Ciara?'

Little fizzing bursts of nerves like fireworks in my stomach, then. Like how you get, maybe, in the moment before asking a girl out. The words are very simple and very hard. Now that they're poised and ready to drop, I really don't want to say them. Equally, I really do. Even if they dissolve in the space between us.

'I love you, Dad.'

He looks flustered. More than usual, even.

'Do you know where the remote control is?' he says.

I bring it over to where he's sitting.

I see he's holding a piece of paper, then, and it says 'THE MAN'S NAME IS MARK' in Ciara's neat girlish hand. And it's almost funny because I'm thinking about the evening last week Mandy and I were discussing this trip at a bar overlooking the harbour. The water was fluttering its million golden eyelashes under the lowering sun. I was all set for the big reconciliation with Dad. I even let Mandy convince me everything would be OK. Because I knew it could be our last chance to talk.

THE MAN'S NAME IS MARK.

Almost funny. Just give me a minute. I'll laugh then.

LOVEBIRDS

Chris Connolly

Chris Connolly's work has appeared in, among others, Southword, Carve, Boston Literary Magazine *and* The New Guard Review, *and had been broadcast on RTÉ Radio 1. Since 'Lovebirds' was published, he has been working on a novel about obsession, somewhat obsessively.*

And if he did hear he gave no indication of it, and later she would wonder about this above all else.

Well you can take your ridiculous birds with you.

She shouted it at him as he leaped down the steps that dropped from their front door to the street, his arms stretched rigid by his sides as he stormed away, the heavy rain instantly soaking his shirt.

She watched him hastening down the street and away from her, fully expecting him at each moment to stop and turn back – or at least to look back, to show some sign of hesitation – until finally he disappeared from sight. She considered going after him or shouting something more to draw him back to her, but instead she closed the door and went back inside, tearful but too angry to cry. She drank tea in the living room, repeating the argument in her mind over and over, unable to sit still for any period of time.

As the day wore on – one more wasted Saturday – her restlessness was replaced with an angry lethargy. She lay wrapped in a blanket on the sofa and stared idly at the television. From time to time she heard the discordant chirping coming from the kitchen. It was a sound he had convinced her she would get used to, though even after a year she hadn't, but until recently the gesture itself had outweighed any annoyance that came with caring for two exotic and clamorous birds.

Friends, when she had told them, reacted with puzzlement. It was the strangest of gifts, but he was oblivious to the extravagance of it, endearingly proud of the statement it embodied, and this only added to the mystique of things. She softened quickly to the idea of it: two star-crossed lovers understood only by each other, the sole members of a secret and amorous club, and the birds a totem of their love. It was all very dramatic and romantic, and he moved in with her a few weeks later.

But lying on the sofa now, hearing their sporadic chirping, the birds seemed to represent other things.

For a while, and in particular the last few weeks, an air of frustration had crept into the relationship. They seemed ill at ease with each other, gentle bickering often overflowing into more serious arguments, the last few weekends marred by their disputes. The latest had been as baseless as the others – at least on the surface of things – but had grown through the morning and into the afternoon until finally it erupted into vicious and hurtful accusations on both sides.

He left then, in a hurry, forgetting even his coat and muttering something about last straws and the end of things, saying he wouldn't be back.

'Well go then,' she said as he was leaving, and he turned momentarily to say something more to her. She was surprised at the bitterness in her tone and noted the look of genuine hurt in his face. She waited for him to speak – to shout, to react – but he simply shook his head and left.

Perhaps attempting to hurt him further, perhaps attempting to draw him back into the argument so he wouldn't leave – she would wonder about this later, would be consumed by it – she followed him out to the top step.

'Well you can take your ridiculous birds with you,' she shouted before he gradually disappeared into the mist of rain. It wasn't unusual for their arguments to end like this, but it was a running joke of theirs how inept he was at storming off, typically not making it out the door or more than a little way down the street before stopping and returning, either to continue the argument or to seek a resolution. And each time she would welcome his return, though usually hiding the fact, never willing to be seen to give in.

And so she was surprised that this time he hadn't returned, hadn't even looked back at her as he left, and it made her feel angry and helpless and sorry all at once.

As she lay prone on the sofa that evening her phone seemed to stare at her from the coffee table, taunting her. She wondered who would give in first; she resolved not to let it be her and waited for him to return in person or to call her. It occurred to her that perhaps in his haste he had left without his phone, but a search of his coat and then table-tops and other spots discounted the possibility. Still, without his coat or anything else she gauged that he would have to return soon: where else could he go?

She waited, and evening turned to night, her anger increasing with the changing light before slowly giving way to worry. Finally she relented and dialled his number, not knowing what to expect but steeling herself for a continuation of hostilities, prepared for the possibility of either his continuing anger or his remorse, prepared to respond to either with an amplified sense of her own misgivings and, following this, her own remorse and forgiveness. Perhaps then, she hoped, they could salvage the remainder of the weekend.

She dialled his number and waited. As it rang the sound of the birds' chirping seemed to intensify and ring along with it from the kitchen. She felt another pang of worry when there was no answer – worry for his well-being, firstly, it not being like him to remain incommunicado, but also for their relationship. She was reminded of her comment about the birds.

It was his gesture from those initial stages of love – excessive though it may have been – that she had used to hurt him, and flippant as the comment was she felt an overbearing need to retract it, to rectify the situation.

She dialled his number again, the tension of the day's turmoil seeming to drain away, replaced now by sorrow and a resolve to apologise, to let him know how much she loved him.

Later, when she thought of the moments that followed, she would wonder at the strange workings of the mind, at how anger can turn to regret and then back to pure rage and heartbreak within the space of a few minutes, how fragile and unreliable affairs of the heart can be.

The phone rang and rang. She pictured him staring at it somewhere, seeing her name light up on the screen but still angry enough not to answer. She felt the guilt mount, and then the worry when still she heard nothing.

She continued to redial his number, over and over, obsessed now with the act itself, and when finally, unexpectedly, the ringing stopped and the phone was answered it took her a confused moment to register that it was not his voice on the other end, that it was the voice of someone else, a female voice; it was a woman who had answered his phone.

Unable to speak, not knowing how to react – feeling, in fact, that she was in some way intruding on something – she hung up and burst into tears. It all seemed horribly clear. It explained their recent difficulties, explained why it had been so easy for him to leave her earlier that day. And she understood instantly that the voice – sounding young and alert, whoever it was – was the voice of a woman taking a situation into her own hands, knowingly answering his phone and speeding along the dissolution of his relationship to hasten and cement the beginnings of her own. It was the dreaded other woman.

She wondered how long it had been going on.

She was trembling when her own phone rang just a moment later. It would be him this time, trying to remedy his predicament, either denying or apologising for his betrayal. But it was clear in that moment that it was the end of things, that things for him had obviously been over for some time – for however long he had been seeing this other woman – and that now it was over for her too, revealed to her in the cruellest of ways. She felt humiliated, betrayed, wronged, and foolish now at her feelings from just a few moments before of having wronged *him*.

She let the phone ring.

She felt floored by the moment, unable to fully believe what had just happened, and she made a promise to herself not to answer, to let him stew in the guilt she was sure he would be feeling, not to allow him any morsel of opportunity to exculpate himself.

It was this nascent sense of betrayal that accompanied her uneasy slumber and throughout the night – in a state of strained half-sleep – the incessant chirping of the birds in the kitchen seemed to be mocking her.

Later, she would recall and dissect the day in excruciating detail; the argument itself, each word exchanged, the image of him striding away from her; the hours that had followed and the places that her mind had arrived; the phone-call, that voice on the other end of the line; her sudden hatred of the lovebirds and their song, obscene and mocking symbols of duplicity.

Later, in her torment, she would try and arrange each aspect of these things in her mind.

It wasn't comfort that she sought, much less redemption; her mind, broken now like her heart, would be unable to allow any cathartic understanding of events. There were too many things to consider, too many uncertainties and each one more shattering than the last – no way to know with any conviction which was the most troubling, the most despicable.

She would be haunted by the argument, by its needless beginning and its petty nature. And by the stubborn determination she had felt not to search him out after he left, the afternoon spent swearing not to be the one to capitulate.

The facts of the accident would haunt her, too.

The details of it were pieced together over the following days like a slowly unfolding horror story – that it had happened mere minutes from their home, mere moments after he had disappeared into the rain; that she had lain on their sofa hating him as he lay alone in the road, wet and broken.

And later in the day, while she had been so consumed with the playing out of the game, he had stayed unidentified in the hospital, being worked upon in vain. This thought would plague her, as would the fact that later that night when her pride finally allowed her to dial his number he was still alive, that had she not been so quick to doubt him, to accuse, she would have realised that the voice answering was not some other woman, but a nurse seeking only to identify him – that he didn't need to die amongst strangers.

And she would be immersed in the sickening knowledge that she had spent his last moments denouncing and reviling him, and by her complicity in both the fact and the nature of his demise.

These things would weigh endlessly upon her.

But it was the lovebirds, that ultimate symbol of his affection and love, which would remain the most sordid reminder of the day. It was the words she had used that would follow her through time, never far away – *ridiculous birds* – and the nagging uncertainty of whether he had heard those words.

It would fester along with everything else, incessant and unanswerable, tearing into her core. Even after the birds themselves ceased to be she would continue to hear their sounds – sometimes mocking, sometimes mourning.

And if he did hear the words he gave no indication of it; this she would wonder about above all else, the immoveable anchor in a cold sea of grief.

2014

DANCING, OR BEGINNING TO DANCE

Sara Baume

Sara Baume was born in 1984. Her short fiction has been published in The Stinging Fly *and* The Dublin Review. *Since her Hennessy short story was published, she won the 2014 Davy Byrne's Short Story Award, and her debut novel,* Spill Simmer Falter Wither, *was published by Tramp Press in early 2015.*

We queue.

The door is still locked, so the queue isn't moving forward. Instead, it moves backward, stealthily growing from the end, person by person. They come on the soles of their shoes from the direction of town, or on horse-powered wheels from the direction of the suburbs. They cross the staff car park to join us. We are standing along the windowless side of the building. The yellowed plasterwork against our backs, a confetti of chewed gum and smoked cigarettes beneath our soles. We chew gum and smoke cigarettes as we queue. We glance impassively around ourselves. To our left, there's a sorry huddle of shabby bungalows. To our right, there's a repurposed industrial estate. It consists of a second-hand furniture warehouse, a fireplace showroom, a camping supplies store and a couple of vacant units. In one shuttered window there's a pink-haired troll holding a tiny placard. BACK IN 10 MINUTES the placard says.

We queue.

We chew. We smoke. Our impassive glancing rarely reaches upward. We are not used to seeing things above the level of the roof gutter on the windowless side of the building. The business of the sky keeps itself from here, from us and our business. This air space belongs to the pigeons and crows. Aeroplanes veer round it. Helicopters hover elsewhere. Sometimes rain clouds descend to shed their load, but today the sky has obligingly parted so that we might see a misdirected object trailing across the grubby blue. Distant, but coming slowly closer.

We queue.

We lift our heads. Even the bowed heads lift. The bowed heads belong to those who still queue in fear of being recognised by neighbours, acquaintances, former colleagues, old friends. Faces to the concrete footpath, they're trying to think of a cryptic explanation as to how they ended up here on this day, queuing. The bowed heads also belong to those wearing blazers instead of tracksuits. Those who arrived in cars with more than two doors and central locking. Those sporting an authentic Iberian suntan. And if these groomed and glowing queuers fail to bow their heads in humiliation, we turn our pasty scowls upon them. We hurl them daggers with our eyes.

We queue.

We hold our social security cards against our hearts. We hide the numbers from sight as though they are the credit cards we're no longer allowed to use. We bite a nail, twist a strand of hair around a fingertip, scratch an old insect bite until it itches afresh. We stop short of nose-picking; we are debased enough as it is. We raise palms to shade eyes and squint into the parted sky. Now the flying thing is close enough to see it's a hot air balloon, and we've never seen a hot air balloon before. The enormous envelope is covered in bold coloured bands, and the bold bands appear to be precipitously tilting. We think it looks as though the hot air balloon is crashing, or beginning to crash, but we don't mention anything to one another. Instead we tell ourselves this is just the ungainly way in which they fly.

We queue.

We carry bags, keys, mobile phones, rain jackets, books, umbrellas, babies. On the ground, there's a scattering of children too old to be carried, too young to be sent to school. The loose children fidget and snivel and kick the ground, ball their fists and stamp their soles. We watch and wish we were as free to vent our small volcanoes of impatience without disgrace. S'NOT FAIR! they cry, S'NOT FAIR! S'NOT FAIR! And even though we feel like fidgeting and snivelling and kicking and balling and stamping too, even though we want nothing more than to punch the yellowed plasterwork and cry I KNOW IT ISN'T FAIR! I GOT A GOOD LEAVING CERT! I HAVE TWO DIFFERENT DEGREES! IT WASN'T SUPPOSED TO BE LIKE THIS! we do no such thing. We swallow our volcanoes, suppress our disappointment. We implore the children to look beyond the level of the roof gutter. We point at the stumbling balloon and tell them it's a fallen piece of space, the brightest of the stripy planets.

We queue.

Between our concrete footpath and the tarmac car park, there's a grassy verge, lush from several consecutive days of drifting drizzle. The front door is still locked, but the natural world refuses to stop and wait with us. The grass of the grassy verge continues to grow. Weeds prod through the fissured tarmac. Wildflowers defiantly bloom. To our left, the closest bungalow has a row of bushes lining the driveway and although they are drab little specimens of treehood, we know that they are growing too. There are net curtains in the bungalow's front facing windows, angel figurines on the sills. And as we queue, the curtains rustle and twitch. The angels fix us with their dead eyes and stare.

We queue.

Eighteen to sixty-five, we queue. Pimples to wrinkles through stretch marks to pattern baldness, we queue. T-shirts and sneakers to cardigans and loafers through jeggings and gilets, we queue. And as we queue, we keep a polite distance from those either side of us. We may be comrades but we are not friends. We know we are slightly better than one another. We do not attempt to open a book. We do not plug our ear holes with headphones. We do not play games on our old-fashioned phones. We turn our pasty scowls upon anyone who does, anyone who has yet to understand: you must be alert, you must be sentient. You have to experience every second of this discomfort. You must bear every ounce of this shame.

We queue.

Now the queue's growing end snakes as far as the fireplace showroom. As we light new cigarettes and crunch the sugar shells from fresh pellets of gum, we pinpoint people we know or partly know or used to know. Neighbours, acquaintances, former colleagues, old friends. We wonder how they ended up here. We wonder how inscrutable their explanation is. Now a man raises the shutter of the second-hand furniture warehouse and a pair of athletic youngsters arrive at the camping supplies store for a day's paid work. They do not appear to notice the hot air balloon. They do not appear to notice us. They hasten past as though we are queuing for a cholera cure. They know that here but for the grace of God queue they.

We queue.

A Jack Russell with an undocked tail trots from the suburbs, dodges through the traffic, crosses the repurposed industrial estate. He finds a lolly stick in the car park and stops to lick the stained end. He reaches the grassy verge, prostrates himself to roll wildly amongst the clover. He scratches his back with almost obscene enjoyment. Now we wish we were so free as the Jack Russell instead of the children. We wish we had a Jack Russell's responsibilities. A Jack Russell's freedom of expression. A Jack Russell's stupid enthusiasm for the humble things he finds beyond the wet of his nose.

We queue.

The front door opens and we begin to shuffle. Shuffling is the only appropriate way for queuers to move, just as slouching is the only appropriate way for queuers to hold themselves. All together we stub out cigarettes, gather up children. The queue moves slowly forward. The open door is a rectangle of alluring light. As we shuffle and slouch in faulty unison, a pigeon settles on the gutter's edge. He preens himself. He kicks tiny pieces of dead moss and dried sludge down on our heads. He taunts us with his chatter as he preens and kicks. *Queue queue,* he says, *queue queue, queue queue.* We do our best to ignore the malevolent pigeon. We look past him to where the hot air balloon is close enough now to see a head above the basket's rim. And maybe arms and maybe hands. And maybe they are waving and maybe they are flailing. We cannot tell. But we do not wave back. We do not flail.

We queue.

Now the Jack Russell picks himself up from the grassy verge as if to follow us. But he doesn't follow. He begins to chase his undocked tail and jump and jump and jump. And it seems almost as if he is dancing, or beginning to dance. Now on the road beyond the car park, a Polo Golf with a foreign registration plate stops to ask a woman on the footpath for directions. The woman lifts her elbows into the air. She swoops her hands and sways her shoulders. And it seems almost as if she is dancing, or beginning to dance. Now we are certain the hot air balloon is in trouble. It's low and close enough to hear the roar of the burners and a voice shouting, maybe hello and maybe for help. We cannot tell. But we do not shout back. We do not help.

We queue.

And as we queue, the telegraph poles and pylons grow. The tower cranes and chimneys grow. The lift shafts of unfinished apartment blocks grow, as though they don't need us any more. The wind turbines relentlessly spin, as do the horse-powered wheels of passing cars, as does the world. Our teeth continue to decay. Our cells continue to mutate. We continue to breathe. And as we do, particles of floating dirt collect in the fine hair of our nostrils, but we don't try to touch them; we do not dare. And the pink-haired troll in the vacant shop unit resiliently holds his placard up. BACK IN 10 MINUTES the placard says, but we know now that he will wait forever.

We queue.

And the hot air balloon, crashing after all, crashes. The enormous envelope crumples into the car park. The propane tanks split and gas spews out. The burner coughs its last and the man in the basket catches fire. He leaps and twirls in yellow flames. He staggers to the verge. He rolls in the grass, just like the Jack Russell. And all together we think to ourselves how it seems almost as if he is dancing, or beginning to dance.

But still we queue.

We have to queue, we must queue.

We do not dance, we cannot dance.

We have to sign on, we must sign on.

CIRCUS MUSIC

Elizabeth Brennan

Elizabeth Brennan's stories have been published in Crannóg *and* Verbal Magazine*. She was shortlisted for a Hennessy Emerging Fiction Award in 2011 and again in 2014. She was shortlisted for the Trevor Bowen Short Story Competition 2012 and the Over the Edge New Writer of the Year Competition 2009 and 2010.*

The windows of the abandoned house look like empty eye sockets.

'Let's go back,' Aidan says.

You laugh at him. 'Coward.'

You are both eight years old and it is your first time at the abandoned house. You've given your mother and his older sisters the slip to make the journey from the village across the fields.

You go inside and Aidan follows, as you knew he would. You pick your way over bricks, plaster and rotten wood. Up above you see gaps in the floorboards of the second floor. At the foot of the stairs Aidan forms his mouth into an 'O' and exhales like a reverse hoover. But he follows you upstairs too.

In one of the rooms on the second floor there's a lonely beam that leads to a window. You say you're going to walk it.

'Don't,' Aidan whispers. His fear makes you want to show off your daring. You place your right foot on the beam and put your weight on it. Aidan makes a little noise behind you as you bring your left foot around to the front and press down.

Your body feels balanced, faithful, strong. You focus your gaze on the sky framed in the window in front of you. As you walk you're half aware that you're humming the circus tune. You feel light, and your arms and legs tingle with an energy you've not felt before. You feel like you could take off out the window.

It is only when you get to the other side you realise your heart is beating fast and your T-shirt is wet with sweat.

'Wow,' Aidan says. His eyes and mouth are dark circles on a white background. 'That was like magic.'

Pride rushes through your veins. You grin and take a bow.

After you've both been to the abandoned house to play a number of times, Aidan still doesn't like it. He says he's sure it is full of evil spirits.

'That's crap,' you say. 'There's no such thing as spirits. Or ghosts. Or God even.'

'There is a God. Why did you say that?'

'OK, there is a God,' you say, because you don't know if there is or not and anyway Aidan looks upset. He's always going on about his mother being in heaven.

Even though you give in he doesn't speak to you for two days.

When you get older your mother sends you to the all-girls convent school in town. This school is filled with psychotic groups of girls, high on deodorant spray and nail polish fumes. They watch you with one sarcastic eye, stripping you down to your pants with the snapped elastic, making you feel disgusting, pimply, contagious.

And suddenly it's as if you have locked-in syndrome. You'd like to speak, to join in, but it's not possible. Because you fear the collective eye of the group that is so powerful it could peel your skin off.

The rules have changed and you're the only one who wasn't told. You feel like you're experiencing the loss of something big, though you have no name for it.

You hang around with Aidan in the evenings and at weekends. Every time you go out with him on a Saturday night it seems that one of his friends wants to shift you in a dark corner. But with all the kissing, groping and panting, you feel nothing.

When the disco lights pick out Aidan's face he looks reproachful.

He says, 'You don't have to shift them all, you know.'

You and Aidan still go to the abandoned house sometimes. If it is sunny, you sit on the steps of the front porch. But most of the time you go upstairs. You sit where the floor is still intact, looking out a window and across the fields to the village. You drink beer and swap information about the bands you like and the people you both know.

The May you are both sixteen, Aidan tries to kiss you up at the house.

You push him away. 'No,' you say.

'Why not?'

'Because we're friends.' You don't tell him he is your only friend.

'But you're friends with all the others too.' He's petulant, a little boy.

'I'm not,' you say.

He puts his hand on your arm and leans towards you. You get up and go downstairs and out the front door.

He doesn't follow.

When school finishes for the summer that year, you get a job as a waitress in Treacy's, the pub in the village. You know the chef

Gavin from around. He's older, twenty-one or two, and he has no problem criticising you for everything.

'Little tomboy,' he calls you, which you like and resent at the same time.

You sweat a lot in the pokey kitchen. It's hot work, but Gavin's nearness is also a reason. You get the odd shuddery trickle of sweat between your breasts and down to your stomach. And one night when you get home from work, you peel off your clothes, lie on your bed and think about Gavin. It's the first time you've ever thought about a boy in this way and it surprises you.

After work on a Saturday night in mid-June, you leave with Gavin by the back door. He grabs your arm and draws you back towards him. His kiss gives you a feeling of falling into deep mud rather than crashing into a pile of sticks, which is what you're used to with Aidan's friends.

After that, you're nervous and excited going into work. You try not to show it, to keep things normal. But Gavin follows you into the walk-in fridge or grabs you in the corner of the kitchen and kisses you.

The first time you actually do it, back at Gavin's house, you feel strange afterwards – confused and tired. But as you do it more, you get used to the flat feeling when it's over. But sometimes the build-up is fun, and anyway it's his groan you're waiting for, his shudder. You've done this to him and it makes you feel powerful.

You and Aidan have always bounced back from your arguments. You still see him that summer, though not as much as before. You don't tell Gavin about when you're with Aidan because you have a feeling he doesn't like Aidan. You also don't tell Aidan about Gavin, because you don't tell anyone. Gavin is six years older and if your mother found out she'd go mad.

One evening you and Aidan are up at the house drinking a naggin of whiskey and talking about this and that. Aidan is being odd, like he's angry about something.

Then he says, 'You're a slut, do you know that?'

You stare at him. His eyes look unfamiliar, glassy and fierce.

'What did you call me?' you say.

'It's what *everyone* calls you.' He gives you a kind-of sneer and raises the naggin to his lips.

'Don't call me that name again.'

'Slut,' he says.

You grab the naggin from him and throw it out the window. There are a few seconds when you look at each other, waiting for the sound of shattering glass. But it doesn't come.

After that you ask your mother to tell Aidan that you aren't in when he calls over. You tell her that Aidan has changed, that he's into drugs. You listen in your room as she says, 'I'm sorry, Aidan. She's not here.' This happens three times before he stops calling.

The first time she sends him away, you watch him walk back down the path, his head bent, his hands in his pockets. You realise that Aidan makes you feel heavy inside.

But being around Gavin gives you a piece of the sky you didn't know you could have. Every day you walk a thin line between excitement and anxiety. You know that one false move could end it all. But the energy that hums in your veins, the sensation of taut lightness to your body – these things make you feel like you can do anything.

Gavin comes into the kitchen and says, 'There's a love-sick pup out in the bar looking for you.' It's a Wednesday in late July, just before Treacy's opens for lunch.

The expression on his face gives you a sick feeling in your stomach. He yanks the tea towel off your shoulder and starts to dry some pots.

You find Aidan sitting in one of the booths.

'What do you want?' you say.

'Will you sit down a minute?' he says. You stay standing.

'Ah, just sit down,' he says. 'Please?'

You glance in the direction of the kitchen door and sit on the edge of the seat opposite him.

He says, 'I just want to say sorry about … what I said. I just want to be friends, I promise …' He looks at you with an uncertain smile. You almost smile back.

An almighty crash comes from the kitchen, as if something large and metallic has hit the tiles. You stand up.

Aidan glances over his shoulder. 'Jesus,' he says, 'what's going on in there?'

'Aidan, you need to go now,' you say. You don't look at him.

'I will if you tell me we're friends.'

'We're not.'

'Aw, come on …' he says. He holds out his hand.

You walk away, leaving his hand suspended, his smile beginning to teeter.

For the rest of the shift, Gavin hardly talks to you. Without saying a word, he throws out plates of steak and mushrooms for you to serve. You decide you were right not to shake Aidan's hand. You're angry with him for coming to see you at work. What did he think he was doing?

'Order!' Gavin shouts, though you are standing in front of him waiting to take the plates out to the bar.

You wonder if Gavin wants to end it between you. Why can't Aidan just leave you alone? If he would just disappear, you think. If he would just die.

Then it happens, in the first week of August. First he is missing and the guards ask you if you know where he could be. The only place you can think of is the house.

Up at the house they find Aidan, a novel by Raymond E. Feist and several empty cans. When they tell you that he fell from the second floor of the house to the floor below, you don't understand it. How did it happen? Who pushed him?

No one, they say. He just fell. He was alone and intoxicated.

For a number of nights after this, you have trouble sleeping. When you do sleep, you dream of watching Aidan from behind as he walks unsteadily along a beam. There is no sound, only dead silence. When you wake up your heart is beating fast and your T-shirt is damp.

You go to a music festival with Gavin in the last week of the summer holidays. Being around Gavin is good because he never talks about Aidan.

Aidan is the only thing your mother wants to talk about, and half the village for that matter. Everyone seems to be looking at you funny, perhaps in sympathy, but sometimes your mother's look is hard with unasked questions.

You see a lot of the bands at the festival that Aidan wouldn't have liked. And it's only in the early morning hours, when you're drunk and stumbling about on trampled grass and cold soil, you let yourself think about him.

And you tell yourself you didn't push him off the beam. You weren't even there.

SOME RANDOM STORY

Sean Coffey

Sean Coffey was born in Gillingham, Kent in 1959 and was returned to the Irish Midlands in 1965 for further development. In 1981 he graduated from the University of Limerick as an electronics engineer. In 1997, with his partner, Gleigh, he helped create a new human resources being, Caombin.

Begin then.

Begin? Make a start. Where. OK. She needed randomness for her work, an art-work. She said she wanted something to happen at random, and asked could it be done. I told her it could be done, but as for randomness, what sort did she want? Yes I was being literal, but she was pretty. And I was an engineer after all. Ours is a literal kind of world. I told her the best I could achieve for the money on offer, which was zero, was pseudorandom.

Explain.

Numbered balls and a lottery bucket can't easily be replicated in software. The probability space gets too big too quickly. Much easier is to write a program that generates numbers that appear random. Like the decimal digits of *pi*. Every time *pi* is calculated the result is the same, but as they appear, the numbers never repeat in a cyclic fashion. Pseudorandom. Randomness generated by an unseen predictive engine running in the background. Like God in the world, if you're that way inclined.

You're not?

No. It's all truly random, what happens.

Like how you met her?

Indeed. A vacancy in our house to be filled, an ad in the paper, room for rent. How many people read the ad? How many people came to look at it? I wasn't even there when she arrived and took it on the spot. Random fate.

You got involved.

A nice way of putting it. I'd always wanted to be a creative myself, she gave me a way in. She asked me to help with a work she was doing, it needed electronics. And randomness. She hadn't thought through the randomness part. That's where we connected.

Describe the work.

What she had in mind was a white plinth a metre and a half square, on which would rest thirty-six ceramic spheroids. Flattened spheres, that is. These to be hollow, mainly white, but speckled, each different. Like eggs, yet not. The visual trope was that these objects would agitate occasionally, like an egg might just before hatching. Only ever one at a time, and at random. She'd worked out how to induce the agitation, she'd drill out the spheres and insert small metal slugs. An electromagnet hidden beneath in the plinth would activate momentarily and trigger movement. What she needed was the control electronics to actuate thirty-six spheres with the requisite randomness.

What did you make of it?

It sounded affecting. Like what Art should be. I was more concerned about getting it to work, to be honest. The engineer again.

So the randomness?

The spheres would be controlled by a microcontroller, a single-chip computer. The choice was between Arduino and Raspberry Pi. I know, the names, all very touchy-feely. There was pseudorandom number generation software available for both. Freeware. But that's when I had my epiphany.

Your epiphany?

I realised that pseudorandom wouldn't be good enough. It would undersell what she was trying to express. Undermine the integrity of the piece. It had to be the real thing.

Did she agree?

After I'd explained, yes. She really bought into it. She could see exactly where I was coming from. It couldn't be anything else.

So how did you achieve this true randomness?

Cleverly, I think. A flat-screen TV would hang in the exhibition space, displaying just static, electromagnetic noise in the atmosphere. A fixed camera would take images of the static, which would be passed on to the Raspberry Pi. First they'd be rendered into pure black and white, then each pixel would be interrogated for its state, zero for white, one for black. This would form a vastly long binary number, which when converted to a decimal would produce a truly random stream of digits. What we both really liked about this was that a major source of static is cosmic microwave radiation left over from the Big Bang. So the eggs would be agitated at the whim of the primal seed of the universe. It was exactly the sort of *thoroughgoingness* we were looking for.

We?

It was we by then.

And the camera and TV would become part of the art work?

Precisely. The rest was hidden, the Raspberry Pi and the interface to the electromagnet array. We debated camouflaging the wire that ran from the camera to the computer with tubing, maybe vacuum cleaner hose or something. But we decided it would look gratuitous. It was wire that carried the images, so let the wire be seen.

Were you pleased with the result?

We were.

But there were reservations?

Not about the work itself, but rather the public's engagement with it. I lost count of the number of times I saw people come, stand, look into the room, see the eggs, then go on their way again without having witnessed an agitation event. Completely missing the point. In the end I altered the software so that the agitations occurred more often, virtually continuously, in fact. We neither of us were happy with this because originally the periodicity was set to be random too – anywhere between one and ten minutes. But what could we do, people's attention spans just weren't up to it.

What were they given by way of elucidation?

A panel of text was set at the entrance to the room briefly outlining how the randomness was being generated. She had originally planned to write more, but in the end we decided it wasn't necessary. The work alluded to more in its actuality than we could ever hope to explain in words. It was Art, in other words.

But try and explain it in words.

The rocking of the spheres was suggestive of a hatching egg, a birthing. I think that's key. Coupling that to the primal cosmic randomness causing it, you had, what should I call it . . . an elegy to being, perhaps. Yes, an elegy to that.

How was it received?

Well. She was invited to show it at a major city gallery. Not bad for a nobody from a provincial town.

But the piece changed.

It did. It developed. As a result of the first showing. We really wanted to reintroduce the random timing. But we knew this would cause problems, people not staying to properly witness the work. So we came up with an idea. She would do the witnessing. She would sit and watch for them. She would become part of the work. Or me, when I had the time. We'd note down which had agitated, and at what time interval. Anybody looking into the room, and it was a room, the gallery space, would see a person sitting focused intently on these apparently immobile objects. Then we had the idea of generating a graphic representation of what was happening. So she did a sketch of the spheres and screen-printed up multiple copies on art-grade paper. On these we'd illustrate the movements and time intervals. Each one would be unique. And for sale.

You made money.

We did. It was a good print to begin with, but when spiced with the actuality of the happenings, it really went. Everyone got a little bit of true randomness for their lives.

You said you did some of the witnessing. What was that like?

Difficult for the first half hour or so. But then it became mesmeric. Your whole being became focussed, waiting for the next event. It was totally distracting.

What was the longest sitting you did?

I only did the one, actually.

Just one?

I was busy. I was working.

Do you feel bad about that now?

No. What happened was, I think, inevitable.

So you maintain. When you say working?

I was writing by then. Small pieces. Short stories.

So having inveigled her into her art you left her stranded there. At the mercy of the random.

Now you're losing it. Ask me more. Ask me about Zurich.

If I must. Zurich?

The Art Forum Gallery in Zurich. She got Arts Council funding to show it there.

Why Zurich – you've never been to Zurich.

I was too busy. I couldn't go with her.

That's not what I mean.

I know. But it was in Zurich that her problems started, her withdrawal. In some ways I blame the gallery, it was their suggestion that she actually stay in the room. Live in it twenty-four hours a day. But then they weren't to know how fine a line she was treading. She stopped taking records of the agitations. She simply sat there and gazed at the spheres. It was three or four days before anyone suspected something was wrong. She'd stopped eating, stopped communicating. I got a call from them saying she was behaving oddly. The rest you know.

Remind me.

When she was forcibly removed from the room she became agitated and violent. She was repatriated and had to be institutionalised. She continues to resist treatment up to the present, and only manifests calm when allowed access to the piece, which has been set up in the hospital. I visit and sit with her on a regular basis, but have so far been unable to penetrate her apparent catatonia. And there we have it. End of story.

Too trite.

The End.

So be it. But Zurich was lazy, a faux pas. *The name of the gallery was obtained from Google, no doubt?*

Indeed. I had to throw something completely random in just to point it up – what you're trying to do isn't working.

I don't know what I'm trying to do.

Oh come, come. Trying to assuage your guilt perhaps? Trying to sterilise the facts by passing them through the autoclave of creative expression, maybe? Trying to re-forge what was already a forgery so that it might become the truth again? I can do this all day, if you like.

Crystallize. I wanted to crystallize it. So I could hold it up, see it, see through it. See through myself.

From the seed of an individual's experience a story grows that somehow crystallizes into a universal truth – some bull like that?

Something like that.

The word seed is also ascribed to the initial number loaded into a pseudorandom number generator. But of course, you know this, don't you. It's just the sort of clever conceit you'll try to use to pull this mess together.

You don't trust me, do you?

No. No writer is to be fully trusted. By themselves, especially.

Touché.

Maybe you should just tell the other story, the one you know to be true.

This isn't what I intended.

Tell the story.

OK. We were in our mid-twenties when we met. She was a mature art student, aiming for a career in graphic design. I was an electronics engineer and frustrated creatively. I turned her head with my talk of Art. Projecting my ambitions, I suppose, so that I might live creatively, vicariously, through her.

You convinced her she could be a creative artist.

She had it in her, she had the skill, the eye, and the soul. A tortured soul, perhaps, and maybe that helped. At the time. Thirty years ago.

But not anymore.

It always catches up, the crap we inherit. There's no outrunning it. Turn, face, confront, overcome, or not. In this case, not. The room we created together became a trap for her. Exposed as she'd become in her pursuit of Art she was too raw to handle the random vicissitudes. She's fallen in thrall to them.

She no longer creates.

She was a painter. An oil painter, a good one, perhaps a very great one.

She no longer creates and now you write about it. Inglorious, would you say?

Never trust a writer.

You should have watched the spheres for her, with her. Instead you stepped back. You took up your pen and left her to it. Which brings us to this story, for want of a better description. Was there ever such an artwork?

There was, not hers, it was someone else's, a random acquaintance. I did help with the controller design. But the rest was fiction, the quest for randomness and what followed. That was artifice.

Artifice? One feeble, overextended metaphor?

Not quite so feeble. The room, our relationship, the work, our creativity, the world, outside, for the most part uncomprehending. The danger, the exposure of the artist.

The betrayal. The abandonment.

All there, implicit.

But you ran out of patience. Zurich.

Weariness sets in. Tired of meaning, tired of engineering meaning into the world. In a pseudorandom way.

Back to that again. I feel an ending looming. You simply can't help yourself, can you.

It's a writer's condition.

No. It's the reader's condition, the human condition. If there's an ending, it can't all be random, can it.

HENNESSY LITERARY AWARDS

List of Winners

1971

Patrick Buckley, Kate Cruise O'Brien, Desmond Hogan, Vincent Lawrence, John Boland, Dermot Morgan, Liam Murphy

1972

Fred Johnston, Ita Daly, Maeve O'Brien Kelly, Patrick Cunningham

1973

John Flanagan, Niall MacSweeney, George O'Brien, Brian Power

1974

Donall MacAmhlaigh, Dermot Healy, John McArdle, Ronan Sheehan

1975

Edward Brazil, Ray Lynnott, Lucile Redmond, John A. Ryan

1976

Robin Glendinning, Ray Lynott, Ita Daly, Dermot Healy, Thomas O'Keefe, Sean O'Donovan

1977
Denis Byrne, Michael Feeney Callan, John O'Leary, Joseph Nesson

1978
Patrick Doyle, M. J. Lally, Jim Lusby, Andrew Tyrrell

1979
Mary O'Shea, Alan Stewart, Patrick McCabe, Harry McHugh

1980
David Irving, Paul Hyde, Deirdre Madden, Michael Harding

1981
Briege Duffaud, Catherine Coakley, Gabrielle Warnock, Elizabeth O'Driscoll

1982
Eoghan Power, Anne Devlin, Rose Doyle, Anne Gilmore

1983
Maurice Power, Jim McCarthy, Brigid Flahery, John MacKenna

1984
Mary Morrissey (writing as Frances Dalton), Ronan O'Callaghan, Vincent Mahon, Bill Hearne

1985
Shane Connaughton, John Grenham, David Liddy, Brian Lynch

1986
Peter NcNiff, Keith Collins, Andrew E. Duffy, Colm Ó Clubháin

1987

Mary Byrne, Geraldine Meany, Áine Miller, Mairide Woods

1988

Dermot Bolger, Maire Holmes, Ivy Bannister, James Leo Conway

1989

Joseph O'Connor (New Writer of the Year), Julian Girdham, Sam Burnside

1990

Colum McCann (New Writer of the Year), Maeve Kennedy, Mary O'Malley

1991

Ted McNulty (New Writer of the Year), Cathy O'Riordan, Colm Keena

1992

Mairide Woods (New Writer of the Year), Sheila O'Hagan, Mike Philpott

1993

Vona Groarke (New Writer of the Year), John Galvin, Mary Arrigan

1994

Martin Healy (New Writer of the Year), Marina Carr, Noelle Vial

1995

Eleanor Flegg (New Writer of the Year), Kerry Hardie/Iggy McGovern, Michael Taft

1996
Gerry Beirne (New Writer of the Year), Martina Devlin, Iggy McGovern

1997
Micheál Ó Conghaile (New Writer of the Year), Rosita Boland, Aidan Rooney-Cespedes

1998
Paul Perry (New Writer of the Year), Philip Ó Ceallaigh, John O'Donnell

1999
Liz McSkene (New Writer of the Year), Alys Meriol, Fiona O'Connor

2000
Geraldine Mills (New Writer of the Year), Kieran Byrne, Pat Maddock, Desmond Traynor

2001
Mary O'Donohgue (New Writer of the Year), Philip Ó Ceallaigh, Ronan Blaney

2002
Alan Monaghan (New Writer of the Year), Patricia Beirne, Lindsay Hodges

2003
Seamus Keenan (New Writer of the Year), Sinead McMahon, Jennifer Harrington-Sexton

2004
Terry Donnelly (New Writer of the Year), Laurence O'Dwyer, Dermot McCormack

2005
Jennifer Farrell (New Irish Writer of the Year), Maria Wallace, Owen Dwyer

2006
Katherine Duffy (New Irish Writer of the Year), Ronan Doyle, Majella Cullinane

2007
Valerie Sirr (New Writer of the Year), Michael O'Higgins, Mary Madec

2008
David Mohan (New Writer of the Year), Kevin Power, Eimear Ryan

2009
Madeleine D'Arcy (New Writer of the Year), Michael O'Higgins, Olive Broderick

2010
Siobhan Mannion (New Writer of the Year), Eileen Casey, Afric McGlinchey

2011
Niamh Boyce (New Irish Writer of the Year), Barbara Tarrant, Viv McDade

2012

Jessica Traynor (New Irish Writer of the Year), Ruth Quinlan, John O'Donnell

2013

Brendan McLoughlin (New Irish Writer of the Year), Sean Kenny, David Cameron

2014

Sara Baume (New Irish Writer of the Year), Simon Lewis, Henrietta McKelvry

THE HENNESSY LITERARY AWARDS

List of Judges

1971 Elizabeth Bowen, William Trevor

1972 Brian Friel, James Plunkett

1973 Seán Ó Faoláin, Kingsley Amis

1974 Edna O'Brien, V. S. Pritchett

1975 Brian Moore, William Saroyan

1976 Alan Stillitoe, Aidan Higgins

1977 Melvin Bragg, John McGahern

1978 John Braine, Mary Lavin

1979 Julia Ó Faoláin, John Wain

1980 Bryan MacMahon, Penelope Mortimer

1981 Heinrich Böll, Terence de Vere White

1982 Jennifer Johnston, D. M. Thomas

1983 Victoria Glendinning, Benedict Kiely

1984 Molly Keane, John Mortimer

1985 Bernard MacLaverty, Robert Nye

1986 Frank Delaney, Judy Cooke

1987 Douglas Dunn, John Montague

1988 David Marcus, Ian McEwan

1989 Piers Paul Read, Brendan Kennelly

1990 Clare Boylan, Desmond Hogan

1991 Fay Weldon, Neil Jordan

1992 Wendy Cope, Hugh Leonard

1993 Penelope Lively, Ita Daly

1994 Beryl Bainbridge, Dermot Bolger

1995 Edna O'Brien, Joseph O'Connor

1996 Justin Cartwright, Deirdre Madden

1997 Roddy Doyle, Patrick Gale

1998 Micheal O'Siadhail, Jennifer Johnson

1999 Marina Carr, Colm Tóibín

2000 Colum McCann, Andrew O'Hagan

2001 Anne Enright, Ola Larsmo

2002 Patrick McGrath, Bernard Farrell

2003 Patrick McCabe, Bernice Rubens

2004 Frank McGuinness, Ronan Bennett

2005 Philip Hensher, Mary O'Donnell

2006 Glenn Patterson, A. E. Markham

2007 Éilís Ní Dhuibhne, Douglas Kennedy

2008 John Boyne, Sally Nichols

2009 Paula Meehan, Carlo Gébler

2010 Paul Durcan, Derek Johns

2011 Giles Foden, Deirdre Purcell

2012 Rupert Thomson, Claire Kilroy

2013 Theo Dorgan, Peter Straus

2014 Martina Devlin, Xiaolu Guo

HENNESSY HALL OF FAME

2003 Dermot Bolger

2004 Joseph O'Connor

2005 Patrick McCabe

2006 Colum McCann

2007 Frank McGuinness

2008 Anne Enright

2009 Hugo Hamilton

2010 Neil Jordan

2011 Sebastian Barry

2012 John Boyne

2013 Dermot Healy

2014 Deirdre Madden